DINO EGG

Charlie James

Illustrated by Ned Jolliffe

BLOOMSBURY

First published in Great Britain in 2008 by Bloomsbury Publishing Plc
36 Soho Square, London, W1D 3QY

Text copyright © Catriona Wilson 2008
Illustrations copyright © Ned Jolliffe 2008
The moral rights of the author and illustrator have been asserted

A CIP catalogue record of this book is available from the British Library

ISBN 978 0 7475 9226 6

All papers used by Bloomsbury Publishing are natural, recyclable products made
from wood grown in well-managed forests. The manufacturing processes
conform to the environmental regulations of the country of origin.

Printed in Great Britain by Clays Ltd, St Ives Plc

1 3 5 7 9 10 8 6 4 2

www.bloomsbury.com

For Lindsey

Contents

PROLOGUE

OK. Here's a question:

An egg hatches into a dinosaur on your kitchen table. Do you:

a) Scream for help and run for the hills as fast as you can?
or
b) Hide it from your mum under a pile of socks and try to keep it as a pet?

Well, to Bill, my six-year-old brother, the answer was obvious:

OPTION B!!!

Was he a complete idiot? Well, yes — but he thought it would be fun and that everything would be just fine.

And so it was . . . until Joe, our arch-enemy, became suspicious. And *then* who do you think Bill expected to sort it out?

ME.

Chapter 1
BILL is BORED

It all started on the first day of the summer term.

It was 7.02 a.m. Outside, the rain was sloshing down in heavy grey sheets. Inside, the words were raining down like hail in a thunderstorm. The Finn family was suffering from a classic case of Back to School Blues.

Now, Mum swears that some people never suffer from this disease. According to her, they bounce out of bed, dress themselves in neatly labelled clothes and trot off happily to school having eaten a healthy breakfast and found all their games kit – *including their gum shields.*

Well. That is Them and this is . . . *Us.*

Get the picture? You see, it's tradition. Mum and Dad have been getting us back to school late on the first day of term ever since Stacey was five. She's now twelve, so that's seven years – or *twenty-one terms* – of missing the early-morning bell! No wonder they look stressed. We've offered to make it easier for them by skipping the first day of school and going back on the second, but they didn't seem that keen.

So as per usual, the pressure was beginning to mount. I was burning the toast; Dad was in the garden shed cooking up his latest fishy recipe (he's a fish-food manufacturer obsessed with creating the world's finest fish food); and Mum was gently encouraging Stacey from her bed.

'STACEY FINN!' she yelled. 'If you don't get up *this instant*, I'll be VERY CROSS!'

'But I'M STILL FAST ASLEEP!' shrieked Stacey from upstairs. 'And anyway, I don't need breakfast. I've eaten two Easter eggs!'

'Chocolate?' shouted Mum. 'No wonder you have spots! Your body is a temple. Instead of filling it with sugars, fats and salts,' she continued, her voice throbbing as she clasped a packet of porridge oats to her breast, 'you should nourish it with

Omega 3 for brain power, protein for energy and calcium for bones!'

There was a short silence as Mum broke off, all misty-eyed. Sighing, I started to scrape the charcoal off my low-salt, reduced fat, high-fibre toast. Mum must be Cattlebury's number one organic health food freak. She believes that she only has to feed us healthy food to turn us into geniuses – but it hasn't worked yet. If our bodies are temples, Stacey's is a shrine to crisps, sweets and fizzy drinks.

Fortunately, before Mum could say any more, she heard a faint chirruping sound coming from the kitchen table.

'Cheep, cheep,' it went. 'Cheep, cheep, *CHEEP*!'

'OK, boys,' Mum snapped, wheeling round, 'who's changed the ring tone on my mobile phone?'

'Not me,' soothed Bill, winking at me. I instantly went on Red Alert.

'Oh, for goodness' sake,' grumbled Mum, 'when will you two boys grow up? Ned, stop fiddling with your toast and eat your boiled egg.'

'But Mum,' I protested, 'there's a funny pink kiss mark on its shell. I bet Stacey's been meddling with it.'

'Of course she hasn't. That egg's organic. It'll be

fine – *unlike* your sister if she doesn't get dressed this minute! Now *excuse* me!' And with that Mum swept out of the room and stormed upstairs to do battle with Stacey.

As there's no point in arguing with Mum-in-a-Mood, I reluctantly picked up my spoon.

'TAP! TAP! TAP!' I went on the shell.

'TAP! TAP! TAP!' it went back.

Bill sniggered and shot me an evil grin. Trust him to play a trick on me on the first day of term. Casting him a dirty look, I gripped my knife firmly.

'Crack!' it went.

'Ouch!' squealed the egg.

Bill dived under the table.

Furious, I lifted the edge of Mum's hand-knitted tablecloth and glowered at him. 'Bill, what have you done to this egg?'

My brother cowered there, as white as a shampooed sheep. 'N-nothing,' he stammered. 'I promise. I found the egg going cheep in the cellar this morning . . .'

'The *cellar*? What were you doing down there?'

'Well, I was bored. I woke up early, saw the door was open and decided to snoop around.'

I gritted my teeth. No wonder we were in a mess.

15

My brother might look like an angel, with his blond hair, blue eyes and wide smile, but if Bill's an angel, heaven has a problem. You see, Bill gets bored easily. And when he's bored Trouble follows – Trouble with a capital T. He attracts it like a magnet. And this morning it seemed he had been bored, bored, bored, bored, *BORED*!

'So . . . where did you find this egg?' I asked, trying to keep calm.

'Hidden in an old golf bag next to Dad's duff fish crisps. I thought it was a toy so I put it in your egg cup as a joke . . .' He crept out from under the table. Together we peered at the egg.

'N–Ned,' Bill quavered, stealing his hand into mine. 'If *you* didn't make those noises . . . and *I* didn't . . . then *who did*? Do you . . . do you think we should call Mum?'

I nodded. But we were too late. For just then the egg began to glow and change colour, exactly like a traffic light.

First, the top of the egg flashed red . . .

Then the middle glowed amber . . .

And the bottom turned green . . .

And *after that*, it started to move. It wiggled to the left; then to the right. Finally it began jiggling up

and down in the cup. Terrified, Bill squeezed himself behind the big Swiss cheese plant in the corner, bravely brandishing a rolling pin and a saucepan lid he'd pulled from the work surface. He even managed to ram a steel colander over his head for extra protection. I crouched behind my chair, clutching a long-handled wooden spoon in palms that were damp with sweat.

And then . . .

C-R-ACK!

The shell split open.

Chapter 2
EGGS-PLOSION

Silence.

Some *thing* was clambering out of the egg cup. It had:

1 NARROW HEAD with a **GREEN FEATHERY CREST**

1 ROUND PINK BODY with **PURPLE SPOTS**

2 HUGE EYES Tight shut

1 long WHIP-LIKE tail

3 SHARP CLAWS on every paw

and a **TRULY TERRIBLE** smell!

'Bill,' I squeaked, covering my nose to block out a stench worse than Stacey's hairspray, 'what exactly is that?'

'Well,' said Bill, craning his neck round the pot plant for a better view. 'I'm not exactly sure, but . . . judging from its profile, lower tibia formation and tail, I think it might be a . . . a . . . Tyrannosaurus[1] rex!'

I groaned. Bill is mad about dinosaurs. He may only be six, but once on the subject he sounds like a professional palaeontologist[2] – an expert dino-bore. He spends hours talking about them, drawing them and playing pretend fights with them. He's as obsessed with the wretched things as Dad is with fish, Stacey with clothes and Mum with knitting. But if Bill was convinced we'd just witnessed the birth of our very own Jurassic Park, I was not.

'Believe it or not, Ned,' he whispered, 'the T. rex was the *King* of the dinosaurs – one of the meanest meat-eating machines ever to have walked the planet. According to my books, it weighed eight tonnes, grew up to twelve metres long and might have run as fast as sixty-four kilometres per hour –

[1] Pronounced like this: *Tie-RAN-oh-sore-us*
[2] *pal-ay-ON-tol-o-jist*

that's about *eighteen metres per second*. Its specially-hinged jaws meant that its bite was five hundred and thirty times more powerful than any living creature. Why, it could probably crush cars with its teeth!' There was a pause. 'Hey, Ned,' Bill added brightly, popping his head through the leaves, 'do you think Mum would let me keep it as a pet?'

'No!' I snapped.

'And why not?'

'Because,' I muttered, keeping one eye on The Thing on the table, 'dinosaurs are dead, deceased, defunct, extinct! That is *not* a dinosaur. *That* is a mutant duck!' And feeling rather pleased at having solved the mystery, I picked up my chair and sat down.

'*A duck?*'

'Of course. After all, it has feathers and a crest. And besides, whoever's heard of a pink T. rex?'

'No one, but that doesn't mean they didn't exist,' sniffed Bill. 'Tell you what, if you really think that creature's a duck, why don't you give it your toast?'

I hesitated, but, as I wanted to prove Bill wrong, I picked up the toast and edged towards the creature with my hand outstretched. I must admit it looked rather cute, lolling against the side of the egg cup with its eyes still closed.

'Tch, tch, tch,' I whispered, making the sound that Mum does when she's looking at something small and helpless.

'Tch, Tch, Yum,' replied the sightless dinosaur, obviously thinking the same thing. Then, to my horror, it started to move. First it stretched out its neck. It stretched it out a long, **long** way. Then it stretched out its left leg and then its right. Finally it opened its jaws to show a double row of jagged, white teeth.

'B–B–Bill,' I stuttered. 'Did you see those . . . ?'

'Fangs? Yes, aren't they cool? *Really* sharp. Do you know what that means?'

'That it's a vampire?' I quavered, as the duck spattered great gobs of gooey saliva over the table.

'No,' laughed Bill, emerging from behind the pot plant. 'That it really *is* a dinosaur. You can tell by its teeth. Have I ever told you how they came in all sorts of shapes and sizes? Daggers, knives, pegs, combs, rakes . . .'

But I wasn't listening. I was looking at the dino-duck. It was moving across the table – directly towards us. 'B–B–Bill,' I stuttered, 'w-watch out . . .'

But Bill was too busy talking to listen. On and

on he went. On and on and on and on, waving his hands around and completely forgetting that something strange with sharp teeth was crawling towards him. 'Believe it or not, Ned, some plant-eaters − or herbivores as they are known − had pencil- or spoon-shaped teeth with angled tops so that they could pull leaves into their mouths and chew them more easily . . .'

The creature pulled the remains of Dad's bacon into its mouth and chewed it up along with one of my socks. 'B-Bill,' I whimpered.

'On the other hand, meat-eaters, or carnivores,' he continued, 'had sharp, spiky fangs which were specially designed to tear through skin, rip flesh and crush the bones of their victims. Tell you what, hand me another bit of toast and I'll creep forward and see if I can get a better look.'

'*No way!*' I shouted. 'Bill, don't you understand? That dinosaur doesn't want to eat your bread. It wants to eat *you*!' And gibbering with fear, I leapt forward to save him from becoming the first fine feast of a famished feathered fossil.

Which was a really bad mistake.

For just then, the dinosaur opened its eyes and jumped on to my neck, shouting:

'Mum!'

Chapter 3
NED FAINTS

When I came round I was lying on the floor, staring up at Mum, my face dripping with water.

'What . . . what happened?' I gasped, feeling cold and damp.

'I don't know, darling,' said Mum anxiously. 'Bill said you fainted so Stacey threw a jug of water over you.'

'Yeah, we heard a loud crashing sound and ran downstairs,' gabbled Stacey. 'And there you were, all white and limp on the floor.'

I looked round. The kitchen was empty. There was no sign anywhere of:

a) Bill

or

b) The Thing.

'Ahem,' I cleared my throat. 'Where . . . where's the dinosaur?'

'*The dinosaur?*' echoed Mum.

'Yes. It hatched out in my egg cup. Bill said it was a Tyrannosaurus[3] rex, and it called me Mum!'

Stacey sniggered. Mum felt my head. '*Ha, ha,* petal, this is just your little joke, isn't it? Are you sure you feel all right? Shall I call a doctor?'

'No way,' snarled Stacey, relishing her moment of triumph. Two years older than me and taller when wearing high heels, Stacey *loves* the fact that she's the First Born Finn. She never misses a chance to lord it over us. 'Huh, if you ask me,' she scoffed even though no one had, 'Ned's just trying to get out of school.'

'Well, in that case, it won't work,' said Mum in a completely different tone of voice. 'Talking dinosaurs, indeed. I've never heard such nonsense. Next thing you'll be telling me it's pink with purple spots!'

[3] *Tie-RAN-oh-sore-us*

26

'Well –' I started.

'Well nothing!' snapped Mum. 'Go and clean your teeth and find your brother. I'll meet you at the car in exactly fifteen minutes. If you're not there, you'll find your dinosaur's the least of your problems!'

So as there's no arguing with Mum-in-a-Bait, I went to look for Bill and his new pest – or rather pet. But they weren't in his bedroom.

Or in the bathroom, the playroom, the garden or the downstairs loo. They were in the cellar where Bill was busily making a shelter for the sleeping dinosaur out of an old birdcage.

'Bill, Bill, this is silly,' I said as he hung small mirrors and toys from the bars for it to play with. 'We must tell Mum and Dad what's happened.'

'OK, but not now,' said Bill. 'Mum's too cross and Dad – well, he's far too stressed. Have you noticed how he's even given up talking in fish puns?' I nodded. There was no doubt that our usually upbeat and enthusiastic Dad was going through what Mum called 'a bit of a bad patch'. You see, it's his ambition to create a 'Finn-tastic' (his words) new fish crisp that will not only make the Finn family fortune but will restock the seas with fish. But so far, nothing's worked. Dad had sunk into the

27

deepest gloom. Now, instead of rushing around the house calling us 'Plankton', telling us how 'swimmingly' things were going and cracking the most terrible fish jokes *(example: What would you do if you found a shark in your bed? Sleep somewhere else!),* he spent his time sighing over weighty reports on falling haddock densities and declining cod-to-hake ratios.

'OK,' I promised, 'I won't say anything. But what happens if it escapes?'

'It can't,' said Bill, with a knowing wink. 'I'll lock the cellar door, keep this key in my pocket and hide the spare in the deep freeze. Mum and Dad will never think of looking there. Don't worry, Ned. I'm not *stealing* the keys, just *borrowing* them to protect an Endangered Species. This little creature will be as snug as a bug in a rug. There's a nice breeze coming in from that broken window and it has loads to eat and drink when it wakes up. It'll be fine.'

And, sure enough, our little pet did look cute and comfortable tucked up in an old blanket with some water in a shallow plastic bowl along with half the contents of the fridge. But I was still uneasy.

'Bill,' I said, trying not to squirm, 'before I fainted,

did you hear . . . a voice, saying, *"Mum!"*?'

'No!' Bill turned round and looked me firmly in the eye. 'Ned, dinosaurs *don't* talk.'

'No, and they don't live either,' I muttered.

To begin with Bill's plan worked well. In next to no time, we were crammed into our car, crawling our way to school via the usual traffic jam. Stacey was listening to her music and Mum and Dad were far too busy arguing about which route to take and who had or hadn't filled up the car with petrol to listen to us. This was just as well, for Bill was desperate to tell me everything he knew about dinosaurs. Huddling close to me on the back seat, he rummaged around in his bag and produced this book:

Dino Facts
By Professor Bron T. Saurus

I blinked with alarm. It was full of brightly coloured pictures of dinosaurs, all of which looked rather large and frightening. The one of the T. rex looked the most frightening of all. But Bill didn't seem to mind. 'I *love* this book,' he smiled, 'and the website's even better. Believe it or not, Ned, dinosaurs are *really interesting*. Listen!' And before I could beg him to stop, he started to read the following out loud:

Fun Facts
The word 'dinosaur' means 'terrible lizard' – even
though the dinosaurs weren't lizards.

'So what were they?' I hissed.
'Huge scary reptiles that lived on land for about one hundred and sixty-five million years,' exclaimed Bill. 'That's *ages*!'

'Were any of them pink?'

'Well, I don't know . . . hang on . . .'

He leafed through the book until he found what he was looking for.

Dinosaurs came in ALL shapes and sizes, but we often think of them as having HUGE bodies and tiny brains. This made them

    a) ugly (unless you were another dinosaur!)

    b) stupid

    c) strong and dangerous and

    d) very, very hungry.

'That's true,' laughed Bill. 'But the Professor's got this next bit wrong, hasn't he?'

Conclusion: PHEW! Thank goodness those dastardly dinosaurs are dead! Otherwise they would have eaten us, squashed us or pecked us to death!

'Great,' I muttered, feeling as cheery as wilted spinach. I'd only been up for one hour, five minutes and ten seconds, but my worry list was longer than our new pet's tail. I mean, if that creature *WAS* a dinosaur, how were we to:

feed it,
hide it or
water it?
AND
(most important of all)
COULD IT BE TRUSTED NOT TO
GOBBLE US UP?

And with these happy thoughts, we arrived at school.

Chapter 4
FIRST DAY BACK

Does school ever make you feel like a sock in a boil-wash? You go in one shape but come out a sodden, shrunken mess, all fuzzy and frayed at the edges. I only have to sniff that corridor, catch sight of those swing doors or glimpse that long low line of loos to feel the life force being drained out of me.

But today was different. Brackenbridge School had changed.

For one thing, it didn't smell.

Well, it did. But not of that nasty cheap floor polish and loo cleaner. No, it smelt – how can I put it? Fragrant – of lilies and lemons and freshly baked bread.

And it looked flowery too. Where once the hall had been a graveyard for a set of battered Formica tables covered with (unused) textbooks, (lost) clothes, (abandoned) dirty games kit, lumps of (rock hard) plasticine, (broken) rulers, pencils and pens, it was now filled with bunches of fresh flowers and baskets of fruit. The newly painted walls were plastered from top to bottom with posters of . . . happy smiling vegetables and fruit. There was even a big sign hanging above the school stage, saying:

BE BRIGHT!
EAT RIGHT!
BUY RON'S FRUIT AND VEG
TONIGHT!

'What's going on?' I asked.

'Dunno, must be some sort of new health kick,' replied Stacey. 'Hey, check out this photo of Joe Blagg winning the school swimming cup. It's *huge.*'

I groaned. Joe is not what you would call my best friend. Greedy, lank-haired and muscle-bound, he has a face full of pimples and the breath of a garlic press. Going to school with him is rather like sharing a fish tank with an alligator: a snappy short-lived experience which is difficult to survive. Thank goodness I didn't have to sit next to him in class.

But, as I said, *everything* had changed . . .

'Ah hah,' smiled Mr Sprott, as I attempted to sneak unnoticed into the classroom. 'Welcome back, Ned. We've saved you a seat at the front.'

I stared at the empty chair and tried not to hyperventilate. 'Please, sir,' I stammered, 'can't I sit in my normal place at the back? I'm long-sighted . . . if I sit too close to the board, I'll get a headache . . . I'll choke . . . I might even die!'

Mr Sprott sneezed noisily into his handkerchief. 'Hmm, interesting, Ned, but as you are usually half-asleep, I doubt you'll come to any harm!'

'Yeah,' growled Joe. 'If I was the sensitive sort, I'd

think you didn't want to sit next to me — *ha, ha!*'

There was nothing I could do. Sensing the sympathetic (they knew I was dead meat) but relieved eyes of the class on my back (if I had to sit next to Joe then no one else did), I picked my way towards my seat.

That day was one of the worst of my life. When not eating my or everyone else's packed lunch (including Mr Sprott's), Joe relieved his boredom by kicking my ankles, pinching my arm and scrawling rude words over my notebooks. Only when he had threatened to thrust my head down the loo did he explain what his problem was.

'You see, bog brush,' he sneered, 'rumour has it that the head teacher wants us to be *buddies*! Apparently, you're to be a good influence on me and that's why we're sitting next to each other in class! Huh!' he scowled, blasting my face with breath worse than a skunk's. 'With friends like me, who needs enemies? Do what I say, or I'll make you *suffer.*'

For the rest of the day I did my best to avoid Joe. I spent all my free time researching dino facts in the library with Bill. Together, we found the biggest dinosaurs, the smallest, the fastest, the brightest, the dimmest and the longest. We discovered dinosaurs that walked on four legs and on two, dinosaurs with horns, lumpy tails and sharp claws. We even learnt that dinosaurs had relatives – huge prehistoric birds and fish. But although we searched and searched, nowhere could we find one jot of information about our prehistoric pet . . . one that was pink with purple spots, huge eyes, a green crest and a long, whip-like tail.

'Hey ho, we'll just have to surf the internet when we get home,' sighed Bill, closing his book. 'What a pity the dinosaur can't talk. And no, Ned, *for the last time*, it DID NOT call you Mum!'

So as soon as school finished, we dashed home. Whilst Bill stole down to the cellar, I rushed into the kitchen to raid it for food – and had a nasty shock: the Swiss cheese plant had disappeared. All that remained were a few bedraggled leaves edged with tiny teeth marks, some bare stems and a rather grubby pot. I was just about to call Bill when his ashen face popped around the door.

'Ned,' he whispered hoarsely, 'come quick! You won't believe what's happened. The dinosaur – it's *gone!*'

Chapter 5
EGGS-PLANATIONS

'*Gone?*' I echoed.

'Yes, it's eaten every single bit of food and half the cage. I think it escaped through the broken window . . .'

'Don't worry,' I said grimly, 'I reckon I know where it is. Look at the floor.' I pointed to a dusty trail of telltale footprints.

Bill gulped and stared at the remains of the Swiss cheese plant. 'Uh oh, Ned. Did our dinosaur do that? Mum'll go ape!'

'Yes,' I agreed. 'So we'd better find it before she does. Ssh! Can you hear anything?'

Bill shut his eyes and concentrated. A faint snoring sound was coming from somewhere near the window. Tiptoeing towards it, we saw the tiny creature fast asleep on a cushion, half hidden by one of Mum's brightly coloured tea cosies.

'Do you . . . do you think we should wake it up?' asked Bill, nudging me forwards.

I picked up a saucepan. This time I wasn't going to take any risks. 'OK then, on the count of three. Remember, be very quiet. We don't want to startle it. Here goes: one, two . . .'

'THREE!' crowed the dinosaur, jumping up and wagging its tail. 'Oh boy, am I glad to see you! Hello Mum, I'm *starving*! Gimme a hug!'

But Bill beat him to it. 'Ned, Ned – you were right,' he shrieked, clasping me round my neck. 'Our dinosaur can SPEAK! It's a MIRACLE!'

'*Miracle?*' I spluttered, wrenching Bill off only to be half strangled by the dinosaur. It might be smaller than my hand but it had a vice-like grip. 'Have you smelt its breath? This thing's a stink bomb. And let's get one thing straight: I'm *not* its – I mean *your* – Mum!'

'But you hatched me out!' retorted the dinosaur, loosening its hold.

'Yes, but that doesn't mean we're related,' I explained. 'You're a dinosaur and I'm . . . well, a *boy*.'

'So am I!' it replied, cheerfully licking my face.

'But you're pink with purple spots!' I exploded.

'So what's wrong with that? By the way, how come my spots are so much bigger than yours? Do you have them all over your skin, or just on your face? That big white one on your nose looks as though it's ready to burst. Hang on . . .'

'Ouch!' I hollered. 'Get off!'

'That's better,' said the dinosaur, retracting its claws. 'Can I squeeze this one too?'

'N – ABSOLUTELY – O!' I yelled, yanking him off my neck and trying to ignore Bill's sniggers. 'I might have the odd –'

'Very odd,' added Bill.

'spot –'

'or zit,' corrected my brother.

'*But*,' I continued, glaring fiercely at him before turning back to the dinosaur, 'may I *please* point out that you are millions of years old and I'M ONLY TEN!'

'*T—ten?*' stammered the dinosaur, a big tear rolling down his cheek. 'But . . . but I don't

understand. If *you're* not my mum, who is? I mean, who's going to look after me and make sure I don't come to any harm?'

'*Us!*' shouted the ever-helpful Bill before I could stop him.

'US?' I glared at my brother. '*Excuse* me!' Yanking Bill's arm, I dragged him back behind the counter. 'Bill, are you nuts?' I hissed. 'People and dinosaurs don't mix!'

'Oh nonsense,' scoffed Bill. 'That dinosaur won't do us any harm. He's *cute*. Besides, he'll make a great pet. He'll be far more fun than Dad's goldfish or Gran's dog. We can keep him in the cellar or, better still, your sock drawer. It stinks so badly no one will know he's there!'

'But what if he gobbles us up?' I snorted.

'*Gobble you up?*' echoed the creature, who was sitting on the kitchen table, picking his teeth with his claws. 'No way! I'm not a cannibal. Unlike some dinosaurs I'd never eat my family. And I promise you, Mum —'

'Ned,' I hissed.

'OK, *Ned*,' repeated the dinosaur, 'if you let me stay I'll be really helpful. I'll even give you a hand with your homework. I'm brilliant at maths, love spelling and can speak over two hundred languages including Ancient Greek, the dialects of Northern Patagonia, Gaelic and Mandarin. That's why I'm so glad to have someone to talk to at last. I've been stuck in that egg for over sixty-five million[4] years – that's . . .' he took a deep breath, 'three billion, three hundred and eighty million[5] weeks . . . *or* . . . twenty-three billion, seven hundred and forty-one million, two hundred and

[4] *65,000,000*
[5] *3,380,000,000*

fifty thousand[6] days . . . *or* . . . five hundred and sixty-nine billion, seven hundred and ninety million[7] hours . . . *or* . . .' He paused for breath. Bill and I stared at him, our mouths hanging open in astonishment.

'Thirty-four trillion, one hundred and eighty-seven billion, four hundred million[8] minutes,' he hesitated, 'and I was beginning to get just the teensiest, weensiest bit lonely.'

'But hang on, how do you know all this stuff when you've only just hatched out?' I asked.

'Simple: ET!'

'ET?' echoed Bill blankly.

'Evolutionary Telepathy. My brain's like a computer: I simply tune in and up pops all this information – just as if you were watching TV or surfing the net. It's great fun – especially as I have fabulous hearing. I could listen to everything that was going on outside my shell through these little ear holes behind my eyes. Can you see them?' The dinosaur paused, bent his head and pointed a claw to the back of his brow. 'I suppose that's how I kept

[6] *23,741,250,000*
[7] *569,790,000,000*
[8] *34,187,400,000,000*

43

myself going for all these years: I was never bored. I've been a Stone Age football and then mistaken for a potato by Sir Walter Raleigh. I even ended up in the pantry of that French queen who was so keen on cake . . .'

Bill dug his elbow into my ribs. 'Who was that?' he whispered.

'Marie Antoinette,' I replied. 'You know, the one

who had her head cut off in the French Revolution! Stacey's always going on about her.'

'Luckily for me (though not for her, alas),' continued the dinosaur, 'just as I was about to be cracked open, I escaped to America in her chef's pocket – which was fine until I nearly became a cannonball in their War of Independence!'

'Then how come you ended up here?' asked Bill.

'By a stroke of luck. I was lying in some rough grass when the world's worst golfer mistook me for his ball, picked me up and popped me in his golf bag. I've been lying down in the cellar ever since!'

Bill and I looked at each other. We knew who was the world's worst golfer . . .

'So why did you suddenly decide to hatch out?' I asked.

'Because I was lonely,' sighed the dinosaur. 'I wanted to meet my mum and live in a family and you seemed really fun. Oh, I can't tell you how excited I am to have met you. There are so many questions I want to ask!'

'Me too,' I grunted. 'I mean, if you're so smart, how come dinosaurs are extinct?'

'Easy: survival of the fittest. I survived because hey, I'm the best! Though I won't be for much longer if I don't eat something very soon. As I think I might have mentioned, I've been stuck in that mouldy old egg for sixty-five million years and all I've eaten since I hatched out are some vegetables and leaves, a few crisps . . . and this rather yummy sock I found under the radiator. Hmm. Actually that was rather good. Much better than this – *yuck!*' A pair of Stacey's frilly pink pants flew through the air and landed at my feet. 'So, please help me. Otherwise who knows what will happen, and there's so much I want to see and do now I'm out in the world!'

And with this the little dinosaur gave a tiny sob and shrank back under the tea cosy. Bill and I gazed at it in horror. 'Ned, we have to help that poor little thing. It's hungry and it's frightened. It doesn't have a mummy. Go and feed it *at once!*'

'Oh, OK!' I agreed. What choice did I have? I hated to see anyone so unhappy. 'I give in! The dinosaur can stay – at least until we've worked out what to do. Now, what would you like to eat?'

'Well,' replied the dinosaur, suddenly cheering up, 'I don't suppose you have any bark from the Zoolang tree or the Yinabow leaf that grows in the Sporang Desert?'

'No . . . but you can have the remains of this morning's porridge,' I suggested, prodding the grey mess at the bottom of the pan.

'Yum!' said the dinosaur, licking his lips. And before we could stop him, he had eaten not only the porridge, but the pan, and the spoon *plus* . . .

1 jug of milk
2 cartons of orange juice
3 bacon sandwiches
4 packets of oatcakes (complete with honey and jam)
1 tea towel, a newspaper and the entire contents of the kitchen bin.

He even finished Mum's malt extract (and if you haven't ever tasted that, all I can say is: *don't*).

As for his manners, they were the kind that Mum dreams of. He chewed everything with his mouth shut, never spoke with his mouth full and always sipped his water after he had eaten his food. But don't ask me where he put it all. By rights, our dinosaur should have been the size of a house, but when he had finished he still looked exactly the same: small, pink, feathery and cute.

Bill and I, on the other hand, were in a mess. The kitchen floor was covered with a mixture of egg, egg cups, spilt milk, squashed toast and squished bananas and the table was littered with crumbs, empty packets and sticky jam jars. We were just trying to clear up, when we heard Mum's voice in the hall.

'Cooeee! Where are you?'

'Quick,' Bill warned the dinosaur. 'Hide under the tea cosy. Mum'll go mental when she sees this mess!'

He was right. No sooner had the dinosaur dived under the cosy than Mum opened the door. 'Hello darlings,' she beamed. 'How did school . . .' The words died on her lips as she stared round the room. 'OK, boys,' she screeched, 'what's going on? And what,' she added, taking a closer look, 'has happened to my plant? Wait a minute, those are *teeth marks*!! Boys . . . have you been *eating my rubber plant*?'

'Uuuurp,' went the brightly knitted tea cosy as it scuttled across the table.

'*Aaah!*' screamed Mum, jumping backwards. 'What's that?'

'What's what, Mum?' asked Bill, all innocent as the tea cosy exploded into a stink bomb and careered off in the opposite direction. I sighed. I knew that malt extract had been a mistake.

'That . . .' warbled Mum, holding her nose and whipping off the tea cosy. Bill and I gasped. The table was empty.

'Where is it – I mean him?' whispered Bill in alarm as Mum paced round the room, looking under chairs and turning over cushions whilst muttering about 'childish pranks' and how this was 'no time for practical jokes'.

'Clinging to the inside of the tea cosy,' I hissed. 'Look, you can just see his tail! Now I don't care what you think, I'm going to tell Mum the truth!' And so, ignoring Bill's frantic signs and dagger glances, I confessed all.

The only problem was she didn't believe me. Instead, she snapped on her super-sweet smile, hugged me (honestly – was it Hug-a-Mug Day?) and said, 'Thank you, Ned. That's a really . . . original story. I think I understand . . . I've been reading about this kind of thing. There's been a lot

49

about it on the radio . . .' She headed over to her Parenting Bookshelf and started pulling down titles such as: *Making the Most of Your Middle Child; Invisible Friends – How to See Them* and *Boys: Is Grunting Normal?* Leaving her deep in thought, I hid the dinosaur in my pocket and legged it up to the bedroom, closely followed by Bill.

'Do you think she's ill?' he asked, as soon as we'd closed the door.

'No,' I replied, gently stroking the dinosaur. 'Just waiting for Dad to get home before she explodes.'

But it seemed not. After an intense discussion with Mum which we could not overhear, however hard we pressed our ears to the door, Dad, too, became super-nice. He kept ruffling my hair, talking about 'Ned's invisible friend' and giving Mum knowing looks whenever Bill or I mentioned the word 'dinosaur'. It was clear that Mum and Dad thought my problem was an imaginary one that would disappear with time and good parenting. Unfortunately, Stacey was not so easily deceived. Flame-haired, green-eyed and with a boulder-sized chip on one shoulder, our Sis has a radar for seeking trouble. She sensed that Something Was Up and decided to find out What

It Was. As soon as I had gone to bed and the coast was clear, she sneaked into my room.

'Right, duh-brain, I'd like a word with you,' she snarled.

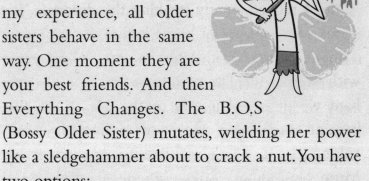

The B.O.S!

PAT PAT

'You . . . do?' I quavered, pulling the duvet right up under my chin as I tried to avoid her eye. In my experience, all older sisters behave in the same way. One moment they are your best friends. And then Everything Changes. The B.O.S (Bossy Older Sister) mutates, wielding her power like a sledgehammer about to crack a nut. You have two options:

1. Run (impossible when you are in bed)
2. Try and bluff your way out.

I tried Option One. 'Ahem . . . bye, Stacey – got to run to the loo,' I grinned cheesily.

'Not if you want to live,' she replied, blocking the door. 'No, you're going to stay here and answer my questions. You see, *I've* been thinking –'

'Have you? Isn't that a bit dangerous? . . . *Ouch!*' I squealed, as Option Two failed and Stacey grabbed my nose (the only bit of me still poking out of the duvet). '*I* want to know what's going on,' she continued. 'How come you're suddenly so interested in dinosaurs? Let's face it, you are behaving very oddly. You've spent all day with Bill; you've invented an imaginary friend; you've been raiding the fridge but are still hungry . . . I mean,' she cooed, suddenly trying another tack, 'it's not as though you can't trust me.' And this from a girl who treats secrets like an airborne virus: something nasty to be spread around as quickly as possible. 'But if you don't, snail brain,' she threatened, reverting to her normal self, 'I'm going to –'

'Oh, Stacey, how sweet of you to say goodnight to Ned,' smiled Mum, popping her head round the door. 'Perhaps you could read Bill a story? He's wide awake and he should have been asleep hours ago! Come on . . . it's his favourite – *Dino Facts* by Professor Bron T. Saurus.'

But though Stacey eventually left me, the dinosaur did not. As soon as my light was out, he crept out of my sock drawer and on to my bed.

'Ned,' he said, snuggling up under my chin like a spotty pink ball, 'I'm worried.'

'So am I.'

'What will happen if anyone else finds out I exist?'

'I don't know, but we'll try our best to keep you secret,' I promised, giving him a large and comforting hug. 'Otherwise, who knows, you might get taken off to a science laboratory, or put in a cage . . .' My voice trailed off as we both thought of the horrible consequences of his discovery.

'Well,' said the dinosaur, trying to be more upbeat. 'They'd *have* to be nice to me. After all, I'm an Endangered Species.'

'Yes,' I said hollowly. 'So am I.'

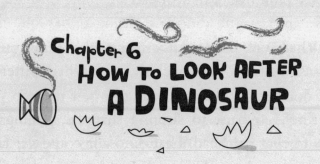

Chapter 6
HOW TO LOOK AFTER A DINOSAUR

I did not sleep well that night.

I kept tossing and turning and dreaming about exploding eggs and giant dinosaurs with huge heads and deadly teeth — although to be honest, that might just have been Joe. Thank goodness, I thought as I finally woke up, it was only a nightmare. This was the twenty-first century. There wasn't — there couldn't be — a dinosaur in my cupboard. When I opened my eyes the sun would be shining, the birds would be singing and . . .

'Wakey, wakey,' interrupted a bossy voice. 'Rise and shine! Time to get up!'

I sniffed. Something that smelt horrible was tickling me under my nose. Peeping through my lashes, I saw the dinosaur, sitting under my chin, chewing one of yesterday's socks.

'Just feeling a little peckish,' he blushed. 'After all, it's 5.16 a.m. and I'm starving!'

'Then go back to sleep,' I snapped, pulling my duvet over my head. That dinosaur could get right up my nose — and it did. 'Ouch!' I yelped, pulling his foot out of my left nostril. 'Can you please go back to bed and *leave me alone*?'

'*Sleep?* But early morning is prime revision time,' tut-tutted the dinosaur. 'I've made a list. If we get cracking now, we can cover everything you studied yesterday. We'll start with your times tables, move on to the present and past tenses of irregular French verbs and then check out volcanic formation and the principles of photosynthesis. If we're lucky, we might even have time to write a ten-point essay plan on "Ancient Rome — The Reasons for the Rise and Fall of an Empire". To be honest, that last one isn't strictly necessary,' he smirked. 'I just wanted to impress Mrs Puggly.' He pointed to the class photograph on the wall. 'She's *so* pretty!'

I stared at my dinosaur in horror. Could it be possible that I was sharing my bedroom with a prehistoric teacher's pet?

Apparently, yes.

By breakfast time, my head was reeling from revision and the effort of learning so many facts in so many different ways. The dinosaur quickly grasped that memory is not my strong point. 'Don't worry, Ned; all you have to do is relax. Come on, we'll try some yoga. Get out of bed, shut your eyes, breathe deeply . . . and stand on one leg. Hmmph,' he sniffed as I picked myself up off the floor. 'Sometimes I despair of evolution. You wouldn't have fallen over if you had a tail. As for your brain, well . . . it just shows that quantity isn't quality. Mine is umpteen times smaller than yours, but I can remember everything. I can't wait to go to school this morning. Tell me,' he demanded, making me dizzy as he wildly chased his tail, 'what's your favourite subject? Chemistry? Algebra?'

'Lunch and free time,' I retorted. 'But I'm sorry; you can't go to school. It's too dangerous. What happens if someone sees you? I'm afraid you'll have to hide in the cellar again. Only this time you

MUST promise to stay there and NOT EAT any more plants.'

'But I'll get bored!' complained the dinosaur.

'Well, why don't you tune into your Evolutionary whatsits and learn something new?'

'Such as?' demanded the dinosaur, looking as sour as Stacey in sensible shoes.

'Well . . . what about these?' And I handed him a book called *Tortuous Tongue Twisters*.

The dinosaur eyed it suspiciously. 'Well . . . I suppose I could . . . but aren't they a bit easy?'

'No way,' I laughed. 'Try one!'

'OK,' he grumbled, licking his lips. 'Plow much oil couth a gum boil boil itha gum boil couth poil oil. There, simple!'

'Yuck,' I cried, wiping a layer of spit from my face. 'That was *rubbish*. Have another go.'

Clearing his throat, the dinosaur sat up and spat out the following words:

'How much wood could a woodchuck chuck if a wood . . .' He paused.

'Woodchuck . . .' he said slowly, 'could chuck . . . Oh, this is hopeless,' he cried, drooling over the page. 'My tongue's far too big and clumsy.'

'Ah, what a pity,' I sighed. 'And there I was,

thinking you could do *everything*.'

'Well, I can,' puffed the creature. 'I just need to practise and relax . . .' Which explains why, for the rest of the week, he spent his days rehearsing tongue twisters whilst standing on one leg in the basement.

But if he was happy, I was not. Hiding a dinosaur in our house was proving every bit as difficult as I had feared. For one thing, he *never* stopped talking, or rather nagging me.

'Have you done your homework, Ned?' he would ask as I took a well earned two-hour rest in front of the TV. 'What's 7 x 316.78 divided by 4? List all the American states and give me five reasons for the causes of the Industrial Revolution.'

And then there was his fixation with water. I don't know what the world was like sixty-five million years ago, but our little dinosaur *loved* getting wet. This was puzzling as, according to Bill's research, no dinosaur ever lived in water (though huge great reptiles called Plesiosaurs[9] and Ichthyosaurs[10] most definitely did). Be that as it may, I was forever rescuing him from the garden pond or Mum's bubble bath or the kitchen sink. 'Thanks,' he'd pant as I scooped him out with a sieve. 'My eyesight's terrible. Unlike you, my eyes are on the side of my head. I can see right round the room – behind as well as in front – but I can't see very far and find distances difficult to judge.'

[9] *PLESS-ee-oh-sorz*
[10] *Ik-thee-oh-sorz*

Admittedly, there were upsides. Our tiny companion was *brilliant* at games, especially hide and seek and chess. Only when it came to practical jokes did my patience wear thin. That dino was a skilful mimic. 'Was that Mum?' I would ask him as her voice (apparently) floated up the stairs saying: 'Dinner's ready, come and get it!' Of course, the dino would just smile. Soon I was Mum's number one kitchen slave. Luckily, she was so thrilled that I arrived in time to empty the dishwasher or lay the table that she didn't mind knitting me ten pairs of socks a week – a relief as old greedy guts ate them as though they were going out of fashion (which Stacey assures me they are). A point which brings me neatly on to the Number One downside of having a dinosaur as a pet:

Food.

According to Bill, our reptile was an omnivore. He ate *everything*.

'Yum,' he said as he gobbled Mum's gardening gloves.

'Mmm, these are good, Bill,' he mumbled as he nibbled the sofa cushions.

'Interesting texture,' he commented as he demolished Dad's notebook of inventions.

Thinking Dad would hit the roof, I once more confessed all.

'Don't worry,' winked Dad, not believing a word. 'I always keep a spare copy of my work. But I don't suppose your *little friend* knows what's happened to Mum's spare knitting needles? They seem to have disappeared . . .'

They had. Our dinosaur had eaten them, along with half a rainbow-coloured jumper (I was thrilled; Mum was knitting it for me). He even swallowed Stacey's hairspray, causing him to whistle for a week. But the WORST was when he escaped into our neighbour's garden and bit a great chunk out of her smart new sundial.

'But why should a dinosaur want to eat *stone*?' I wailed, peering over the fence at the all-too-obvious row of teeth marks.

'Indigestion,' answered Bill. 'He probably needed the stones to grind up Mum's knitting needles. I bet they were a slight mistake, even for him. Listen!' And he pulled out his trusty copy of the Professor's book:

Stones

It is a strange fact that lots of plant-eating dinosaurs swallowed their food without chewing. Instead they gobbled stones and pebbles which banged and rubbed around in their tummies and helped to mash their food into a pulp.

'I'm sorry,' apologised the dinosaur, giving me a big lick. 'I didn't mean to cause so much trouble. As for the fuss last night . . . all I did was sneak a lift in your mum's car to this great big house full of food. Honestly, who'd have thought they'd miss a few fusty carrots and tomatoes?'

I kept quiet. The newspaper's headlines were still etched on my mind:

Yesterday's shoppers in the quaint market town of Cattlebury were shocked to find a huge rat munching on produce at their local supermarket. Eyewitness Mrs Blagg – mother of champion super-swimmer Joe, who also witnessed the scene – gave us this terrifying account: 'I've never seen anything like it. I saw this great big pink rat with purple spots. Then we all screamed and ran away. The police and fire brigade were called but by the time they arrived, that rat had disappeared – and so had all the food!'

Mrs Blagg is currently undergoing counselling.

But it was hard to be cross with the dinosaur for long. He was always so cheerful and happy to see us. As for the food he ate – I simply could not work out why or how he did not grow any bigger. The dino couldn't – or wouldn't – shed any light on the problem and I was too busy looking after him to puzzle it out. I just hoped that, when he did grow, the increase would be gradual and that I wouldn't suddenly wake up to find I was sharing a room with a creature the size of a hippopotamus. But, as he never seemed to change size, I slowly began to relax. Bill even suggested that life was getting back to normal, but I could not agree. Normal for me is:

1. Watching TV
2. Oversleeping
and
3. 'Forgetting' to do my homework

It is *not* practising tongue twisters and being nagged to do my school project by a pet so old he made our gran look young.

Surely, I thought as I tucked the dinosaur into my sock drawer at night, life couldn't get more complicated?

What a silly question.

Of course it could.

So of course, it did.

Chapter 7
THE SUMMONS

The letter summoning me to visit my head teacher, Mr Peaseby, along with Mum and Dad, arrived the next day. This is what it said:

BRACKENBRIDGE SCHOOL
CATTLEBURY
MIDSHIRE

Dear Mr and Mrs Finn,
We urgently need to discuss Edward's future at Brackenbridge School. Please ring my secretary WITHOUT DELAY to arrange an appointment.

Yours sincerely
Mr Peaseby
(Head Teacher)

Mum took one look at the letter and promptly burst into tears. Then she and Dad rang up the school and fixed an appointment with the head for that morning.

But if their reaction was exactly as I'd expect, Bill's and Stacey's was not.

'Are you going to be expelled?' Stacey gloated.

'Can I have your bedroom if you go to prison?' pleaded Bill as soon as we were on our own.

'Prison? Why should I go there?' I snapped. 'I haven't done anything wrong . . . have I?'

'Ooph, I don't know,' mused Bill. 'After all, you have been harbouring a dinosaur . . . isn't that against the law?'

'Well, it's *you* who found it,' I retorted. 'It was your egg! If I go to jail, so do you!'

'Yes . . . but *I'm* only six. *I* wouldn't get into trouble. You're my older brother so everyone will say that you should have looked after me more carefully!' And with a smug smile that made me want to hit him, he whistled his way to the car. I glared after him. I couldn't be sure, but I'd swear there was a halo hovering over his golden curls.

But like it or not, Bill's words had hit home. Was it illegal to keep a dinosaur as a pet? And if so, could I be sent to prison? Or – my stomach churned – *could Mum and Dad*? By the time I reached school, I was too nervous to look anyone in the eye. I slunk my way to the head teacher's office, flanked by a pink-cheeked Dad and a Mum who was close to tears.

'Good luck, son,' Dad comforted, patting me on my shoulder before he knocked on the door. 'Remember, whatever you've done, we'll stand by you.'

Mum licked her handkerchief and dabbed at a spot on my cheek. Unfortunately, as it was a spot, it wouldn't disappear. 'Yes, Mr Peaseby can't be half as bad as you think.'

She was right. He was worse.

Mr Peaseby is a tall, slightly bald man with the neck of a turkey and the fashion sense of a dog basket. He has a pale, eager face with eyes that beg you to like him and a mouth that dares you to try. For though Mr Peaseby longs to be popular he fears our disrespect. As a result, he is not a man I like.

Or trust.

And today it seemed my instinct was right.

Let me explain. Mr Peaseby had spent the whole of last term (and let's face it, the term before that and that *and that*) wearing an assortment of frayed jackets, worn ties and socks and trousers which never reached his ankles. Next to him even Dad – a man who wears kipper ties with rugby shirts – looks smart.

But today Mr Peaseby's socks had gone.

As had his tie . . .

and his jacket.

Instead, our head teacher was wearing flip-flops, a flowery open-necked shirt, board shorts, a hoodie and (I can hardly believe I'm writing this) an *earring*.

Even his bald patch had disappeared – hidden under a shock of bleached hair that had been scraped across the top of his head and greased in place with gel.

'Yo, cool dudes, give me five!' he cried. And holding up his hand he slapped it down towards Mum's, missed it and thumped his bare (and rather bony) knee. 'Drat,' he whimpered, snagging his worry beads in his watch strap. 'I just don't seem to be able to get the hang of that. Still,' he smirked, patting his tummy and checking his profile in a mirror, 'that's the price of fame; though, *sssh!* Don't say I mentioned the F-word, or I shall be giving the game – or should I say, *TV show* – away! Now, sit down and let me tell you why you are here. It's because we, Ned Finn, need *you*!'

I choked. 'You do? Why?'

Mr Peaseby beamed and strode over to a flip chart that was standing in the corner of his room. Turning over a page with a flourish, he said, 'Tell me, have you ever heard of a man called Amor Ron?'

We shook our heads and stared at the picture. It showed a small, tubby man with three chins and a cheesy smile. 'Mr Ron, or *Amor* as he's asked me to call him,' gushed our head teacher, 'is Cattlebury's most brilliant businessman ever. He's made a fortune from distributing vegetables and fruit to every corner of the world. His poster is hanging above the stage downstairs; soon it'll be plastered over every bus, billboard, cinema and TV screen in the country. Which is why we were all so thrilled when he came up with his latest idea: the Loch Ness School Swimmathon!'

'The Loch what?' repeated Mum.

'The Loch Ness School Swimmathon – a new inter-school swimming competition that will take place in Scotland at the end of this summer term.'

'Huumph, sounds a bit fishy to me,' grunted Dad. 'What does he get out of it?'

'The chance to tell the world the truth: that you are what you eat! You see, Amor Ron is a Man with a Mission. He wants to show how, if you buy his fruit and veg, not only will you eat the best produce money can buy, you will also become healthier, brighter and fitter!'

'And how will he do this?' growled my ever-sceptical Dad.

'Through the miracle of reality TV!' trilled Mr Peaseby, clasping his hands together and lifting his eyes as though in prayer. 'Our most bountiful benefactor wants to encourage the *worst* swimmers as well as the best. To this end, he has offered to sponsor a number of short TV programmes filming his mascot – the country's worst swimmer –

learning to swim in the lead up to the Big Race. Thus he will demonstrate how even the most scared, the most witless, the most useless no-hopers can overcome their fears . . . as long as they eat Ron's fruit and veg. Now, what do you think of that?'

Mum gasped. 'What a brilliant idea! The man's a genius! But I don't understand. Where does Ned fit in?'

'He's the hopeless haddock that's to be Amor's mascot.'

'*Ned?*' shouted Dad.

'*Ned?*' squealed Mum.

'*Me?*' I wailed.

'Yes!' nodded Mr Peaseby, almost hugging himself with glee.

'But Mr Peaseby,' protested Mum, 'there must be some mistake. Ned *can't swim*. He won't even try!'

'I know,' agreed my head teacher.

'No, Mr Peaseby, I don't think you quite understand,' added Dad. 'He *hates* water. He never takes his foot off the bottom of the pool and the only time he gets his head wet is in the shower.'

'Exactly. That's what makes him so perfect! Do

you realise the trouble we've had trying to teach him to swim? He's pushed six PE teachers to the brink of a nervous breakdown and our lifeguard swears that if he has to save him from the shallow end one more time he'll lodge an official complaint. So when Amor Ron asked us to nominate the country's worst swimmer, your son won *by a unanimous vote.*'

Mr Peaseby was right. I *loathe* water. Drinking it is bad enough, but as for swimming – *yuck!* I'd prefer to eat a bowl of prunes. I mean, if Nature had intended us to swim, don't you think she'd have given us gills and a tail?

'Of course,' burbled my wise and all-knowing head teacher, 'we understand that you might feel a little daunted by the idea, Ned. But have no fears, I am here. This is a wonderful opportunity for me – I mean you. You'll be famous – a TV celebrity, a star, a household name! And so shall I, or rather,' he blushed, 'so will *Brackenbridge School*. For be assured, I see it as my duty, nay, *my honour*, to be always at your side – a trusty guide who will help, encourage and motivate you to . . . to . . .'

'Swim – huh, good luck!' interrupted Dad, who was becoming just the teensiest bit annoyed by the

gooey way Mum was staring at Amor's photo. 'But Mr Peaseby, even if you do succeed, this plan's a bit ambitious. If I remember correctly, Loch Ness is the chilliest, deepest, darkest lake in Scotland. It's over thirty-six kilometres long and about two hundred and twenty-seven metres deep. How's he going to survive that, let alone the Loch Ness Monster?'

'The . . . the monster?' I quavered.

'Oh, *ha*, *ha*, you don't need to worry about that,' chuckled Mr Peaseby, his eyes sliding away from my face. 'It's nothing but a legend invented by the Scots to attract visitors to their lake – or, as the natives there say, *loch*.' He mopped the spit from his chin and wiped the desk in front of him. 'However, Mr Finn, you are correct. The swim is risky for the novice . . .'

I agreed. That's why I wasn't going to do it. It was time to make my stand. I took a deep breath. 'Mr Peaseby . . .'

'Swimming there,' continued Mr Peaseby, ignoring me as per usual, 'will be a test; a trial of skill, endurance, courage . . .'

And madness, I thought. 'MR PEASEBY!' I shouted.

He must have gone deaf. 'Which is why . . .' he persisted, turning his back to me and pointing theatrically to the next picture on his flip chart, 'Amor has come up with this! Waddya think, Ned?'

'But, sir,' I squeaked, 'that's . . . that's a tomato!'

'Correct, Ned,' agreed Mr Peaseby, miraculously regaining his hearing. 'But not *any* tomato. A specially crafted, totally inflatable, waterproof, bomb-proof, chill-proof, heat-retentive swimming aid made from recycled vegetable matter. It is ecologically sustainable, environmentally friendly and completely biodegradable. All you have to do, Ned, is to put it on top of this . . .' he flicked the page over, 'bright green, skin-tight wetsuit complete with gloves, hood and shoes and bob along the surface of the water for twenty metres to start the race. Not even the Loch Ness Monster will be able to bite through this baby. There'll be nothing to worry about.'

Nothing to worry about? Excuse me. That loch might not have a monster in it, but it certainly had water, and TV star or no, I wasn't going anywhere near it – especially given the timetable. Schoolwork (including my yet-to-be-started-and-therefore-unfinished school project) would be exhausting enough without having to learn to swim in *under ten weeks*.

'Mr Peaseby,' I pleaded one last time, 'this is impossible. I can't do it.'

'Relax, Ned, of course you can. And don't worry, you'll have plenty of help,' cooed Mr Peaseby. 'Why, we've even found you a Buddy: someone who can swim brilliantly; who sits next to you in the class and, most importantly, will represent Brackenbridge School as our Champion Swimmer at Loch Ness. Your Buddy, Ned, is none other than . . .'

I closed my eyes. Please, *please*, I prayed, let it be anyone but . . .

'Joe Blagg!'

Chapter 8
DISCOVERED!

There was nothing I could do.

Nothing.

It didn't matter how much I begged, argued, ranted or protested, no one – or rather no adult – would listen to me. I shouldn't have been surprised. Talking to adults can be rather like speaking to goldfish. They swim around, opening and closing their mouths but half the time you haven't a clue what they're on about. Worse, they don't seem to hear a word you say. Here are some classic examples of what I call Fish Speak:

FISH SPEAK

Example 1

Me:	*But Mum, Joe CAN'T be my Buddy. He's a bully and he loathes me!*
Mum:	*Nonsense. He's told me he can't wait to spend quality time with you and show you his true colours.*

Example 2

Me:	*But Dad, I'll drown!*
Dad:	*Rubbish! You only say that because you can't swim!*

Example 3

Me:	*But Mr Peaseby, learning to swim is taking up all my time. My work is suffering.*
Mr Peaseby:	*Don't worry, Ned; it's so bad already no one will notice. Just make it up in your free time.*

See what I mean? Only the dinosaur was of any comfort.

'Hmm, this is serious,' he agreed, giving me a big lick as he checked my homework in my bedroom. 'You can't have Joe as your Buddy. Why, he sounds as thuggish as a Theropod[11] . . .'

'*The group name for all meat-eating dinosaurs*,' explained Bill, his nose – as ever – stuck inside his dino book.

'. . . as awful as an Allosaurus[12] . . .'

[11] *Thee-ROP-od*
[12] *AL-oh-sore-russ*

'*A nippy, meat-eating cannibal . . .*'

'. . . and as ugly and underhand as an Utahraptor[13]!'

'*A sickle-clawed, carnivorous raptor, who could hack 1.5 m from its prey with a single slash of its 20 cm claw,*' grinned Bill with gusto.

I gulped. Couldn't any of those dinosaurs have flower–arranging as a hobby? But though I might think dinos were a dodgy lot, I couldn't argue with *our* dinosaur's conclusion.

'It seems to me,' he continued gravely, 'that Ned is in Big Trouble and that we have to help him. As far as I can see, there is only one solution: Ned will *have* to learn to swim! So, come on, Ned – change into your swimming things and lie out on that stool. We'll practise the strokes first and then go into the bathroom and teach you how to put your head in the water. Let's go!'

And much against my will, we did.

It was a horrid experience. The stool was hard and uncomfortable. Its legs scraped my knees and the wood dug as painfully into my ribs as the dino's voice into my skull. 'That's right, Ned,' he

[13] *YOO-tah-RAP-tor*

commanded. 'Stretch out your arms, kick your legs and breathe. One, two, three . . . *one*, two . . . three.'

I fell off the stool. Apart from a few splinters and a load of goose bumps, I hadn't learnt anything at all.

Undaunted, Bill and the dinosaur trooped me off to the bathroom. 'Are you sure you need your snorkel, flippers and armbands?' sighed the dinosaur as I clambered into the bath. He was just preparing to rap out some instructions, when Stacey knocked on the door.

'*Oi, you two*, open up!' she yelled. 'I know you're in there so there's no point denying it! It's time to 'fess up and tell me what's going on. Hang on,' she added, rattling the door handle. 'Why are you running *a bath*?'

'I'm feeling a bit . . . poorly,' I bluffed desperately. 'The bath water's nide and hot and . . . I dink I've got a bid od a code . . . *a . . . Achoo*!'

'Well, I don't believe you,' snarled our walking, talking Lie Detector. 'If you don't let me in RIGHT NOW, I'm going to kick the door down. One . . .' she cried, shoving her shoulder against the door. '*Two* . . . two-and-a-half . . . two-and-a-quarter . . . two-and-an-eighth . . . two-and-a . . .'

'What are we going to do?' wailed Bill.

'Hide him under this towel whilst I head her off,' I commanded. 'If you rumple it up on the floor she'll never suspect a thing.'

But it was too late. On Planet Stacey her maths adds up. She knows only too well that:

$$\frac{\textbf{Bill + Ned} \times \textbf{strange sounds}}{\textbf{1 (locked) bathroom}}$$

$$=$$

$$\textbf{SECRETS!!!!}$$

Hearing our whispers she gave the door an extra-hard shove, rammed it open and strode into the room.

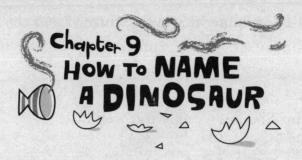

Chapter 9
HOW TO NAME A DINOSAUR

It was love at first sight.

Stacey took one look at the dinosaur (who was still sitting on the side of the bath) and went straight into Major Mother Mode. And what was the first thing she did? Give him a make-over. The dinosaur loved it.

So did we. Before tea our feathered friend had looked like this:

But by bedtime he was transformed into this:

And our problems had just begun.

The first was that the dinosaur shrank as she washed him in the basin.

'Woooah!' screeched Stacey, 'you're disappearing!' And it was true. The dinosaur had shrunk to the size of a bar of soap, when usually he was as large as this book.

Surprisingly, our tiny dino was not at all fussed. 'Don't worry,' he chuckled, slightly embarrassed. 'I always shrink when wet. That's how I've managed to eat so much food and yet stay so small.'

'But why didn't you say anything?' I asked indignantly.

'Well . . .' The dinosaur paused and looked a bit sheepish. 'I've been getting into such trouble that I thought you might stop me from going anywhere near water. And if you knew I was beginning to grow, then you might not want to look after me any more . . .'

'But of course we would,' reassured Stacey, cuddling him tight. 'Oh, Ned, he's so cute. What's his name?'

'Well, I don't know,' I replied, taken aback. 'Normally we just call him "*him*" . . .'

'Or "*The dinosaur*",' added Bill.

'Or "*whatsit's face*",' I finished lamely.

Stacey's face turned a nasty shade of puce. 'You mean, he's been hatched . . . for all this time . . . and you *haven't given him a name*?' she screamed. 'That's so *typical* of boys! Well, if you haven't named him then *I* shall. *I* think he should be called Stacey, after me!'

'*Stacey?* You can't call a male sixty-five-million-year-old dinosaur Stacey,' said Bill in disgust.

'Oh, I don't know,' I pondered. 'After all, they both have sharp claws, a big mouth and a nasty bite!'

Stacey ground the heel of her shoe into my big toe. 'Well, why don't we call him after his species?' she suggested. 'I mean, if he . . . or rather *you*,' she said, turning to the dinosaur, 'are a Tyrannosaurus[14] rex, we can call you Trexy Rex.'

'Yes,' sighed our dapper dino, 'but there's just one little problem: *I don't know.* I mean, I know what type of dinosaur I'm *not*; I just can't remember what I *am*, where I come from or even how big I'll be when I grow up. It's not a very comfortable feeling . . .' He trailed off, a big tear rolling down his face.

[14] *Tie-RAN-oh-sore-us*

There was a short silence.

I stared at the tiny creature and tried not to panic. What if our prehistoric pet grew to be bigger than a Diplodocus[15]? Or a Giganotosaurus?[16] Even if he lived in a bath all day, how soon before he'd be as big as our house?

But Stacey is not a girl to be down for long. She suddenly jumped up, a huge grin on her face.

'I know, let's call you Lucky!'

'*Lucky?*' exploded the dino. 'Why?'

'Because you are!' Stacey was almost hopping up and down with excitement. 'You hatched out in Ned's egg cup, in our kitchen in *our* house. So we're going to find out who and what you are . . . and take you home!'

[15] *DI-plod-oh-kuss*
[16] *Gig-an-OH-toe-SORE-us*

Chapter 10
DINO DIETS

After that, things changed.

Up until then, Bill and I had looked after the dinosaur in a casual, hand-to-mouth (or in his case, dustbin-to-jaw) kind of way that had suited us all well. The dinosaur had been content to live in the cellar or my sock drawer, nibbling on the odd (and in some cases I do mean very odd) piece of footwear and mooching around in my pocket or my school bag. But now, thanks to our new Earth Mother, Things Had to Be Done Differently . . .

Properly . . .

and *On Time*.

For a start, we had to rejig the dinosaur's diet. We now spent all our pocket money on Lucky's food. I say 'we' advisedly, because what Stacey told us to do, she didn't actually do herself.

So, *we* might spend our money on porridge oats and carrots, but *she* spent hers on hair gel and face cream. *We* might be forced (by her) to push the dinosaur (in doll's clothes, sunglasses and a hat) round the garden in her old pram (thus causing Dad to fall off his ladder and Mum to consult her book: *Middle Child Syndrome – The Crisis Signs*), but *she* passed the time curling Lucky's feathers and painting his nails pink. Stacey called this leadership, but *I* called it the typical behaviour of a bossy older sister.

And then Stacey had her masterstroke: the Dino Diary. 'Look, boys,' she argued, 'Lucky is really important – *the* scientific discovery of the twenty-first century. It's essential we keep a daily journal and record every single detail about him.'

'But surely that's too risky?' I protested. 'This information's Top Secret – where can we hide it?'

'Why, in your school project book, of course!' replied our very own 007. 'No one in their right mind would bother reading that unless they had to! It'll be as safe as houses.'

Sadly, when she read my efforts, Stacey was unimpressed. 'It's not exactly Darwin, is it?' she sniffed, her dreams of scientific stardom fading before her eyes.

'No, but then I bet Darwin didn't have to put up with you two scrawling over his notes – not to mention Lucky's footprints!' I protested. And in case you think I might be exaggerating, here's an extract:

DIARY OF LUCKY, THE MYSTERIOUS DINOSAUR

Q: WHat type of Dinosaur is He?
A: We Don't Know – even tHougH Stacey's spent HOURS searcHing websites for clues! However, LUCKY assures us He is NOT:

1 A Tyrannosaurus[17] rex – PHEW! THat T. rex was one of tHe scariest meat-eating Dinosaurs ever! CruncHeD-UP bones Have been founD in its fossiliseD stomacH.
2 A BracHiosaurus[18] – DOUble PHEW! THis plant-eater weigHeD as mucH as ten

[17] Tie-RAN-oh-sore-us
[18] BRAK-ee-oh-sore-us

elephants and grew to twice the height of a giraffe. Imagine having that as a pet!

3   A 40 m long Argentinosaurus[19]. Wow – this might have been one of the heaviest land animals ever to have lived! One of its vertebra measures 1.3 m!

4   A fish-eating Baryonyx[20]. Wouldn't trust it an inch – its smile was just like a crocodile's!

5   A Stegosaurus[21] or 'roof lizard' (an armour-plated plant-eater with a body as big as a bus; a head the size of a horse and a brain as small as a walnut).

6   A speedy egg-eating Oviraptor[22] with powerful jaws and two spikes in the roof of its beak.

7   A defenceless Edmontosaurus[23] (a toothy plant-eater who had to scare off carnivores with loud noises it made by inflating two large flaps over its nose holes).

[19] *AR-gent-eeno-sore-us*
[20] *Bah-ree-ON-icks*
[21] *STEG-oh-sore-us*
[22] *OH-vee-RAP-tor*
[23] *Ed-MON-toe-sore-us*

8 A DIPLODOCUS[24] (a HUGE plant-eater with
   peg-like teeth. It could grow up to 26 m
   long and weigh 10,000 kg. YUCK!
   Imagine sharing a bedroom with that!)

Q: Where was it found?
A: In Ned's egg cup on the first day of term

Q: What does it look like?
A: ~~UGLY, DUCK-LIKE,~~ cute
B: smelly
C: ~~VERY INTELIGANT, INTELLAGINT,~~ Brite.
Height: Half Stacey's hairbrush
Weight: same as my pencil case

Q: What does it do?
A: Sleep, eat, ~~talk,~~ nag, bathe, do yoga and
practise tongue twisters standing on one
leg . . .

Q: What does it eat?
A: Everything!! Anything!!!!

[24] *DI-plod-oh-kuss*

It was true. Even Mum was getting suspicious. How long would she believe we all loved raw Brussels sprouts? According to the Natural History Museum in London, matters would only get worse:

WHAT DINOSAURS ATE EVERY DAY

Tyrannosaurus[25] rex — *75 kilos of meat – that's 1,500 sausages (or 200 packs of bangers!*)*

Brachiosaurus[26] — *450 kilos of plant matter – that's 3,000 apples. (Mum only buys ten a week!*)*

Baryonyx[27] — *25 kilos of fish – that's about 833 fish fingers. (Let's hope it doesn't ask for seconds!*)*

Edmontosaurus[28] — *100 kilos of plant matter – or 1,000 tomatoes. (No wonder it chewed its way through hundreds of teeth!*)*

[25] *Tie-RAN-oh-sore-us*
[26] *BRAK-ee-oh-saurus*
[27] *Bar-ree-ON-icks*
[28] *Ed-MON-toe-SORE-us*
*According to Ned

Euoplocephalus[29]   *70 kilos of vegetables — or 700 carrots. (Bet it could see well in the dark!★)*

Fortunately, help arrived in the nick of time. The next day Amor Ron sent me a free box of fruit and vegetables along with this note:

Dear Ned,

Hope you love swimming as much as eating my yummy fruit and veg! Don't worry about gobbling all this up — I'll send you a new box each week until the Big Race! Must dash now. You're a great mascot — you really ARE the worst swimmer I've ever seen!

Amor Ron xx

Mum was delighted. She *loves* beetroot and radishes and told me it was a real treat to have so much fresh spinach. She even let me keep some in my room in case I felt peckish. But though Lucky now had enough to eat, his improved diet had an unfortunate side effect — a side effect SO repellent

[29] *You-OH-ple-kef-ah-luss*
★*According to Ned*

that I fear that it might upset those of you who are

nervous . . .

sensitive . . .

or easily alarmed.

For I had forgotten one, regrettable fact of nature:

That what goes in must come out, HOWEVER disgusting it might be.

And in this case it was.

VERY.

Very, very, *very* disgusting indeed.

It was Stacey who noticed it first. 'What's that smell?' she sniffed. It was late afternoon and we were upstairs in my bedroom. I was practising swimming strokes on the stool whilst Bill and Stacey were sorting through yet more books and websites in the hope of spotting a dinosaur that might be related to Lucky. He, meanwhile, was sitting on my school bag, checking my homework and nibbling one of my socks.

'Oops, sorry,' smirked Lucky, blushing so pink you could hardly see his purple spots. 'I've had a . . . *little accident . . .*'

We stared at my backpack. My school project book was littered with small oval pellets that looked just like miniature chocolate eggs but were, in fact, the most *horrible* thing you can imagine: *dino poop.*

'Eugh *yuck*!' I exclaimed. 'This is GROSS!! And it's far bigger and stinkier than before. Why couldn't you have done it in the litter tray as normal?'

'Oh, don't worry,' cried Bill, carefully picking up one hard-shelled pellet with a pair of pencils. 'Believe it or not, dino dung's really valuable.'

'*Valuable?* But it's the stuff we flush down loos,' I protested.

'Perhaps, but experts love the stuff. Listen!' And he whipped out his copy of Professor Bron T. Saurus's book and read out the following facts:

Dino Poop

Some palaeontologists[30] spend all their time looking for, digging up and examining dino poop to see what these creatures liked to eat — and it seems they weren't too fussy. One of the largest bits of dung found was 112 cms x 41 cms x 33 cms and weighed 2.5 kilos. It was left by a T. rex in Saskatchewan, Canada. Ouch, must have been painful!

NB: Amazing Fact

Dino poop is very valuable. Some petrified poop (called coprolite) is even sliced up and made into jewellery. Imagine that! Your necklace could be one hundred and fifty million years old. Fabergé, possibly the world's most famous jeweller, even made a cup out of dino poop for Tsarevich George Alexandrovich, brother of the last Russian emperor, Nicholas II. It had a gold and sapphire handle but

[30] *pal-ay-ON-tol-o-jist*

I still wouldn't have liked to have drunk from it, would you?

'Wow,' said the dinosaur, puffing himself up. 'I'm *so* important. Do you think they'll be drinking from cups made from your poop in a hundred million years' time, Ned?'

'No way,' I grunted. 'Nor yours. This *stuff* is going straight into the garden. After all, that's what Glam Gran does with her dog litter.'

'Yes,' agreed Stacey. 'If we hide it in Mum's new flower bed, no one will ever notice that it's there.'

Which is the last time I ever listen to my sister's advice.

Chapter 11
TOMATO SKINS

If things were almost under control at home, at school they were distinctly out of hand. The news that I, the world's worst swimmer, was to be Amor Ron's mascot at the Swimmathon spread like wildfire. So did the news that Joe was to be my Buddy and instructor. *Everyone* was looking forward to seeing me make a fool of myself on TV; *everyone* was wondering how long I'd survive.

Including me.

Which is why, on the morning of the first swim to be filmed, I tried to throw a sickie.

'Mum,' I moaned, 'I don't feel well!'

'Then eat some breakfast,' said Mum-the-Practical, placing a bowl of organic muesli in front of me.

'Dad,' I groaned, 'I think I've strained a muscle.'

'So how come I saw you running round the garden?' he asked. (I'd been looking for Lucky. I couldn't find him anywhere.)

And then the delivery man arrived with Amor Ron's swimming aid and I didn't have to pretend any longer. That costume was the pits: a huge red rubber ball emblazoned with the words *AMOR RON SAYS: EAT FIVE TO STAY ALIVE!* in bright green letters.

The tomato suit had a life of its own.

'Ouch,' yelled Dad as, freed from its packaging, it bounced out and biffed him on the nose.

'Hmm,' said Mum, reading the note. 'It says: *Handle with care, keep away from heat and don't open without reading the instructions.*'

To put the suit on, I had to unzip it down the front and climb in wearing a long-sleeved green wetsuit complete with hood, shoes and gloves. The only problem was the tomato was too big. The bottom of the tomato dangled around my knees, chafing the inside of my thighs. My arms stuck stiffly out from the sides whilst my legs poked out from the bottom like skinny green ski-sticks. Bill and Stacey took one look and burst into laughter.

'You look like a fat scarecrow!' cried Stacey.

'No, Humpty Dumpty!' gasped Bill. 'Don't sit on a wall – you'll fall off!'

But sitting anywhere was almost impossible. When I did, the shoulders of the costume rose up, biffing me on the chin and smothering my head with a ruff of shiny fake leaves which made me sneeze. Furious, I was just struggling to unzip the costume when the phone rang.

'Oh, hello Mr Ron. . . oh, may I? *Amor*,' said Mum, giggling nervously and checking her reflection in the electric kettle. Dad snorted and rustled his newspaper angrily.

'Yes . . . yes, it's here. Ned looks *great*,' she lied, '*cherry* red, you could say . . . in the *peach* – ha, ha – of health, the *apple* of our eye . . .' she prattled on, patting her hair. Dad grabbed the kettle and noisily filled it with water.

Mum paused. 'What's that? You'd like him to wear it to school? Oh, no, no, I'm sure it's not a problem. Ned'll be delighted – it'll save him having to take it off. Absolutely . . . a *fantastic* advert for your good work . . . we're *so* . . .' Mum broke off and stared at the handset. 'How odd – we've been cut off!'

'Harrumph! What did that turnip – I mean *man* – want?' growled Dad.

Mum's face turned the colour of my suit. 'Nothing, really. He just asked if Ned could go to school in his tomato costume, ready for the swimming lesson. It'll save time.'

But not my reputation, I thought as I tried to get into the car.

'Turn on your side,' Mum squealed as she pushed me sideways through the passenger door.

'Curl up your knees!' puffed Dad as he tried to squeeze me in through the boot. 'Jump,' he commanded as he opened the sunroof. 'Stacey and Bill – hold that trampoline steady!' But it was no good. The panels on the sides of my tomato suit were too strong to be pressed flat.

Finally – with the help of two passing neighbours and an arm lock from Mum which made Stacey eye her with renewed respect – I was forcibly stuffed in the back seat. Bill and Stacey squeezed in beside me, sucking their fists to stop themselves from laughing.

Getting out of the car was easier. Dad gave me a gentle push and I popped out and bounced around the pavement like a giant red space hopper. It was *dead* embarrassing. Stacey and Bill laughed so hard they were almost sick. But the worst was yet to come.

'Hurry up, Ned, you're late!' panted Mr Peaseby, running up to us with a smile so bright it nearly gave us snow blindness. 'Your swim starts in five minutes and Amor wants to interview you for TV. Don't worry,' he said, glancing at my face. 'All you have to do is smile, tell Mr Ron how wonderful his fruit and vegetables are and – oh yes, *ha, ha* – be nice . . .' he chuckled nervously, 'about *me* – I mean, the school! Shouldn't be difficult. What do you think . . . good, isn't it?'

I looked round. Brackenbridge School was almost unrecognisable. The stern iron gates were festooned with garlands of flowers, fruits and vegetables. Metres of brightly coloured bunting were hanging from every window and, wherever you turned, you could see small pictures of Joe and me, larger ones of Mr Peaseby and giant posters of our sponsor, Amor Ron.

But Mr Peaseby was anxious about the time.
'Now off you go, Stacey. Your parents are in the
gallery with the rest of the school. Bill, help your
brother. There's a big audience, so we'd better not
keep them waiting. Joe's being interviewed by
Amor Ron right now.'

Sure enough, as Bill and I entered the changing
rooms, we could hear snatches of Joe's words
coming through the double swing doors: '*Sadly, if
you ask me, Ned's lazy . . . useless . . . lacks will power
. . . I'll do what I can to teach him, but hey, I'm not a*

104

miracle worker – just the county's best swimmer!'

Bill curled his lip. 'Don't listen to him, bro,' he said. 'That idiot has an ego bigger than his backside!'

I smiled weakly. Then, pausing only for the briefest of cold showers, I waddled through the swing doors.

Yuck! The stench of chlorine made me shiver. Blinking in the glare of the flashing cameras, I carefully picked my way across the damp tiles to the side of the pool. There was a ripple of applause and the sound of poorly stifled laughter. Amor Ron was not impressed.

'Welcome, Ned,' he beamed icily, bringing his interview with Joe to a close. 'Let me introduce you to the audience. Ned Finn, everyone, is my mascot and the Swimmathon's most unlikely hero – a terrified trout, a panicky plaice who, until today, cod – *ha, ha*, these jokes just keep coming . . .' he wiped his face with a bright pink handkerchief, 'not even flounder in the water without calling out for help. But today – *today*, ALL THAT WILL CHANGE. And why? Because you are what you eat! And according to Ned's mum, Mrs Finn,' he blew a kiss to Mum in the gallery, 'he's already eaten half a sack of my delicious produce as part of his healthy new diet! So, tell me Ned, are you ready to jump in?'

Jump in?

Me?

I stared at the water. Let's get one thing straight: I *never* jump into a pool. Instead, I creep down the steps in the shallow end with my knuckles clamped so tightly round the bars they have to be prized free with a crowbar. I was just wondering if it was possible to somehow avoid this terrible fate when . . .

SPLAT!

I found myself head down in the water in one ghastly, spluttering bellyflop.

'Hurrah!' cried the audience, rising to their feet.

'Oops, sorry, Ned,' said slimy Joe in a voice that echoed round the hall. 'I didn't mean to push you in. Must have slipped on the tiles! Let me teach you swimming rule Number One: how to put your face in the water.'

And with that Joe dived in and ducked me, not just once but again . . .

and again . . .

and again . . .

'*Gettoff*,' I spluttered finally. 'Leave me alone!'

'Not likely, pus face, this is far too much fun,' mocked Joe under his breath.

'Oh, is it now?' said a familiar voice from somewhere inside my costume. 'Hmm, come on, Ned; let's show this bully how it's done.' And before I knew what was happening, I heard a faint humming sound from deep in my tomato suit and I started to move very, *very* fast.

'Lucky, stop!' I whispered as the water whizzed by. 'Slow down! What's going on?'

'Don't worry,' replied the dinosaur. 'I'm hiding in one of the panels of your tomato costume. There was no way I was going to miss the fun. You know how much I love water. So, come on. Stretch those arms and kick those legs. Let's go!'

Up and down the pool we powered. Up and down, then down and up, the dinosaur acting as my very own turbo-charged onboard motor.

'Clunk,' went my feet on the side of the pool.

'Thump,' went my head against the end as we turned once again.

'Bravo, Ned,' cried the audience, going wild.

'I don't believe it,' growled the out-paced, out-

classed and stupefied Joe. And then disaster struck . . .

Lucky, swimming too fast, crashed at top speed into one end of the pool. He tumbled out of my costume into the water.

'Hey, that's a tail,' cried our enemy as Lucky quickly scrabbled back into my tomato suit. 'What's going on?' Joe grabbed my arms and held me fast. 'Show me what it is or you're dead meat. I know you've something stuck in that costume. I reckon it must be an animal. An otter, or a guinea pig, or . . . or . . .'

'Hurrah for our *wonderful* new swimming star, Ned Finn!' cried Amor Ron, rushing towards us, microphone in hand. 'Let's give him a big round of applause. He must be exhausted!'

That was true. Completely dead beat, I paddled my way to the edge of the pool to the sound of loud cheers.

'Ned, you're a hero,' beamed Amor, gripping my arm tightly as he heaved me out of the pool. 'Pure dyna— or should I say *Ron-a*-mite! Can you tell us the secret of your success?'

A hundred pairs of eyes looked at me expectantly. I was dripping wet but I could feel the sweat breaking out on my forehead. What should I say? Being a TV star was even worse than being a tomato on legs. Amor was becoming tetchy.

'Come on, Ned, don't be shy,' he hissed, a hint of steel in his voice. 'Just *answer the question*!'

Once again, Lucky saved the day. 'Of course,' he cried, mimicking my voice perfectly. 'You – *Amor Ron* – were my inspiration. Your slogan is spot on: Be Bright, Eat Right – Buy Ron's Fruit and Veg Tonight!'

There was a gasp, a laugh and a round of applause. 'Well, well, Ned, you are kind, too kind,' smiled Amor to the audience, adding in a voice only I could hear: 'I don't like clever clogs, so next time, make it snappier. Remember, all you have to do as my mascot is swim and praise me and my company. You don't need to break any world records . . .' Turning back to the cameras, he beamed. 'I don't know about Ned, but I could do with a nice cup of tea and a healthy snack. Let's go and warm up!'

And he swept everyone out of the hall.

Except for Joe.

Still in the water, the overlooked swimming ace was slicing his way up and down the pool, practically snarling. For once, the school's champion had been ignored.

'Just you wait, Ned Finn,' he hissed, raising a fist in the air. 'There's something *fishy* going on and I'll find out what it is if it's the last thing I do! I'll expose you on TV for the lousy cheating skunk that you are. You'll be expelled from Brackenbridge School and I, *Buddy,* will be the hero! Just you wait and see!'

Chapter 12
CLASS ACT

The rest of that day passed in a bit of a haze.

The exhausted dinosaur slept soundly in my backpack, whilst I spent my time either being feted as a hero or playing hide and seek during break with Joe — only it wasn't for fun. As for the classroom, I survived sitting next to him by keeping my head down and mouth firmly shut . . . until the dinosaur woke up.

The bell had just sounded for the end of the first period of double maths, when I heard a rustling noise at my feet. Glancing down, I saw Lucky poking his nose out of my bag and looking round inquisitively. Alarmed, I bent down and tried to tuck him back in my bag.

Except that I couldn't; he'd eaten most of it. So not knowing what else to do, I smuggled him into my pocket.

Mr Sprott was distinctly unimpressed. 'Hah, Ned,' he said, peering at me over his spectacles. 'When you have quite finished rummaging around in your bag can you tell me the answer to 8 x 7 *without using a calculator*?'

8 x 7?

I didn't have a clue. But then, I never do. It's a sad fact that I can never remember anything. I can name every character in *Star Wars*; programme the computer or list the top ten goal scorers in the Premier League. But ask me to recall the capital cities of the world, recite my times tables or remember the geographical location of Mount Etna, then no. My mind's a blank. A fact that Mr Sprott knew only too well.

'Come on, Ned,' he snapped, relishing my confusion. 'I'm waiting! Say something – anything – surprise me . . . surprise the class . . . surprise yourself . . .'

'GURGLE!' went Lucky's tummy. He'd

obviously found my school bag as disgusting as malt extract.

'WHAT???' spluttered the teacher.

'Sorry, sir,' I gasped, turning bright pink. 'I think it just slipped out – must be my . . .'

'*BBBBUUUUUUUUUUUUUUUURRRRP!*'

'. . . indigestion . . .' I finished lamely.

Which explains why I spent the rest of the lesson in the corridor and all lunchtime in detention.

Looking back, I blame myself. Struggling to find a way of keeping the dinosaur quiet, I hit upon the idea of feeding him. The only problem was that I didn't have any food. All I could find in or around my desk were shrivelled-up leaves, pencil shavings, rubbers, paper and bits of unwanted textbooks. Lucky obligingly gobbled them all up, but the effect of his diet was dire. For (and again, I apologise to those of you with a sensitive nature) he

Farted in French . . .

Exploded in English . . .

And stank out science.

By mid-afternoon I was beetroot with embarrassment and Joe was mad with rage. 'I'm not

sitting next to that skunk for one more moment,' he yelled, scraping his chair back from his desk as Lucky let off a particularly obnoxious smell. 'It's like sitting next to a pigsty. Ned's a human cesspit.' And for once, the teachers agreed.

That afternoon, I was sent home with a letter.

Dear Mrs Finn,
We are sorry to have to inform you that Ned's habit of burping and passing wind has become so bad that his form has nicknamed their room The Class at Poop Corner. We realise that this might be due to his new diet, but please can you do something or we shall be forced to teach the form outside or (on rainy

days) issue each pupil with a gas mask.
Yours sincerely
Mr Sprott (signed, in the absence of the Head
Teacher, on behalf of every single member of staff)

'It's SO UNFAIR!!!' I shouted at Bill as we made our way home. 'Mum'll go mental when she hears what's happened. I mean, what have I done to deserve all this hassle except try to eat a crummy old egg?'

'Eggs-cuse me,' retorted Lucky, 'my egg was not crummy!'

No, I thought indignantly, but then it wasn't Lucky who was going to end up with egg all over his face at Loch Ness this summer. And though I was truly grateful for his help that morning, there was no doubt that our problems were growing by the minute . . . by the hour . . . even by the day. And when I say growing, I mean just that.

Chapter 13
GREEN FINGERS

When Mum read Mr Sprott's letter she was furious.

In fact, she was *SO* mad she decided to start her own vegetable patch. 'Ned's only whiffing because of his new healthy eating plan. Hmm. Maybe Amor's vegetables aren't all they're cracked up to be. I'd better grow my own. At least they'll be organic!'

But guess where she decided to grow her produce? In the very flower bed where we'd been hiding Lucky's dino poop. And whatever that poop contained it had the most unusual effect on Mum's vegetables. According to the seed packets, these plants should take months to grow. But Mum sowed hers on Monday, watered them on Tuesday and then watched them grow . . .

and GROW . . .

and *GROW* . . .

until, by Friday, they were

SIMPLY ENORMOUS!

Of course, Mum and Dad were delighted.

'Oh, Petal, these vegetables are perfect, just like you!' gushed Dad as he helped her to pull a metre-long carrot from the ground. 'I've heard about having green fingers – but you must have green hands!'

'Thank you,' panted Mum. 'Do you think Ned will lend me his swimming goggles to peel this shallot?'

'Hmm, perhaps,' replied Dad, admiring the (usually) tiny onion that was bigger than a football. 'But isn't it strange how well your plants grow here? It must be something to do with the soil. Why don't I take some samples and find out? Who knows, it could be the start of the Finn family fortune. I might even find a magic ingredient to put in my fish food. As they say – where there's muck there's cash!'

But I would prefer to think that where there's

dung there's worry. For Mum's leeks were not the only things that were growing in our house.

So was Lucky.

Although he could still squeeze himself into my tomato costume, there was no doubt that his tail was longer, his paws bigger and his neck had stretched. He now needed a daily bath to stay small enough to tuck into my sock drawer and even Bill was becoming concerned that we might have to find a larger hiding place for him.

Luckily, before Dad had time to research the garden soil, another letter arrived from Amor Ron:

AMOR RON
RON'S FRUIT AND VEG COMPANY
TURNIP HOUSE
ARTICHOKE BOTTOM
PARSNIPSHIRE

Dear Mr and Mrs Finn,
Congratulations! Ned's swimming lesson last week was a HUGE success. He'll be a great mascot for us, as I gather his school marks are brilliant, his concentration has improved and his homework is done on time. Mr Peaseby says this is due to one thing and one thing only — ME and my brilliant fruit and veg —

the BIGGEST,
the BEST
and the YUMMIEST in the world!
Anyway, we at Ron's Fruit and Veg want to ~~profit,~~ ~~exploit,~~ advertise Ned's success (and ours!!!) by interviewing him live on TV at your house next Thursday. We'd like him to dress up in his cute red

tomato costume (great publicity) and answer some questions about school, swimming and (of course!!) ME!!! The format's simple. All Ned has to do is:

1. Say how much he LOVES my fruit and veg
2. Say how it has HELPED and INSPIRED
    him to swim
3. Eat a couple of platefuls of my DELICIOUS
    AND NUTRITIOUS produce!

Waddya think? Joe Blagg (who tells me Ned is really trying by the way!) will come along as well. If you agree, please sign the attached form and send it back to me ASAP.
Must dash – time is money and money is time. See you at 4 p.m. on Thursday week . . .
Love and kisses
Amor Ron

PS I've just had another 20-carrot gold idea! Why don't Stacey and Bill dress up too? Stacey could be a carrot – perfect with that ginger hair. Bill could be a raspberry. He'll blow the viewers away! I'll send the costumes round tomorrow.

Everyone in the family was thrilled about the interview – even Mum. 'I'm going to be a TV star!' shrieked Stacey, texting all her friends. However, she nearly changed her mind when she saw her

costume: a narrow padded orange tube with a hole in one side for her face.

'I'm going to be famous!' cried Bill, capering around the kitchen dressed as a raspberry in a costume so small he had to keep tugging it below his bottom.

'And I'm going to be dead meat,' I muttered, wondering how we were going to hide the dinosaur from Joe.

I wasn't the only one to be worried. It suddenly occurred to Mum and Dad that Amor Ron might be a bit jealous of Mum's huge leeks and a marrow that was longer than her leg. So, not wanting to upset him, they decided to conceal the veg behind a makeshift screen cobbled together from the washing line and a selection of old sheets, towels and tatty tablecloths. The result looked a bit messy, but we were too busy trying to find somewhere to hide Lucky to help. We couldn't put him in the cellar as Mum and Dad, fed up with being unable to open the door, had changed the locks and pocketed the keys. 'Can't let my old fish crisps fall into the wrong hands,' Dad had laughed.

Which is why, after much discussion, we decided to bury Lucky at the back of my cupboard under a load of Stacey's underwear. 'With luck, even Joe won't dare to rummage through these,' chortled Stacey as she piled her frilly pink knickers over our tiny pet.

But Lucky's luck was about to run out.

Chapter 14
LIVE ON TV

Amor Ron arrived on Thursday at precisely four o'clock. He was as gushing as a burst pipe.

Joe followed, as cheery as a blocked drain.

'Welcome –' began Dad, but Amor was already in full flood.

'What a lovely home!' he warbled as he swept past.

Joe grunted. He had refused to dress up as a vegetable and instead sported slicked-back hair, a large pair of shades and a shiny blue suit that strained round his bulging biceps.

'Hello Carrot Top,' he sniggered at Stacey, as he

stuffed his mouth with a handful of sweets. 'You look terrible. Why weren't you an Ugli fruit? Then you wouldn't have needed to dress up!'

'EEEeee!' squealed Stacey, swinging for him. Joe dodged sideways and Stacey ended up ramming her fist into Bill's padded rear end. Luckily Bill had other things on his mind.

'I wish someone could help me stop my tights falling down,' he muttered, yanking his raspberry-coloured footwear up his legs.

But nothing was going to spoil Amor's day.

'Hi, there,' he cried, his three chins momentarily hiding his parsley-green bow tie. 'Isn't this fun, aren't you excited? We're running late, so let me introduce you to everyone!'

I watched as six large vans emptied themselves of crew who squashed and squeezed into every possible corner of our kitchen. There were people setting up lights and strange white umbrellas, unrolling miles of cables as they went; others were laden with make-up, hair dryers, flasks of tea, boxes of biscuits and crates and *crates* of vegetables and fruit. And as the room filled up, so it became hotter and noisier.

'Welcome —' Dad tried again.

Wham! Dad ducked as he was almost beheaded by the soundman's boom. 'Sorry mate, did you say something?'

'Oh, no . . . nothing,' grinned Dad feebly, retreating to the back door with Mum. My costume began to creak slightly. Was it the heat?

Amor Ron was in his element. 'Great, everyone,' he enthused, rubbing his hands together as beads of sweat dripped down his smiley face. 'Don't forget to sort out your props. Rodney, get shot of those ridiculous Roman blinds and put up the black-out curtains!' Mum looked stricken. Those blinds were her pride and joy and that tear looked difficult to mend. Oblivious as ever, Amor clapped his hands.

'Remember, whatever happens *don't touch this red*

switch!' He pointed to a large red knob labelled 'ON/OFF', mounted on a battered yellow box that was set on the floor at the back of the room. 'That red knob,' explained Amor, 'controls the electricity supply to all the lights, recording equipment and cameras. Press it down and *phht!* Our show goes off the air. No power,' he hissed, glaring at us with hard eyes, 'means no show. No show means no sales, no sales means no money and . . .' he took a deep breath, '*no money means* that I get VERY, VERY CROSS! Geddit?'

We all nodded. We 'got it' all right. No one would risk their lives touching that box. 'Good, splendid.' The manic smile returned to Amor's shiny face.

'Twelve minutes to transmission!' yelled one of the crew, stopwatch in hand, clipboard at the ready.

Suddenly, I felt a nervous tightening of my tummy. This was *it*. I – we – were really going to be interviewed on TV. Stacey pinched my hand for luck and Bill said, 'OK, Ned?' But though I nodded, I could feel my heart pounding in my ears and my throat turning dry. What would happen if I messed things up? If I couldn't answer a question or I spoke too quickly – or quietly? I ran my fingers round my collar of fake green leaves. They were itching more and more in the heat and, though too big, my bright red tomato costume suddenly started to feel strangely tight. Perhaps I should ask someone to cut off the ruff? But it was too late. Amor coughed and spoke again.

'Right,' he said, mopping his brow with a bright yellow banana-patterned handkerchief. 'Let me explain what will happen when we go on the air. First, we'll show some TV footage of Ned learning to swim at Brackenbridge School. Then I'm going to praise Ned, and then Ned will say how he owes all his success to *ME*. Then – facing that camera,' I turned and was glared at by the cameraman in question, 'he'll eat a small plateful of my *wonderful* fruit and veg as prepared by Wendy, our exotic French chef.'

'Oh yeezz,' crowed the cook in her distinctly un-French-like accent. 'First aye will give le pertite cauliflower some stewed prunes, then some boiled cabbaarge and feeen-ally my signature dish . . . *Ratatouille à la Brussels sprouts!*'

'Delicious! What a treat for Ned,' cried Amor as I paled. 'And at the end,' he continued, madly mopping his brow, 'we'll pan the cameras over to Joe . . .' the cameraman rolled his eyes, 'and ask for

127

his advice on swimming and tips for healthy eating!'

'Great,' grinned my Buddy, blowing out some bubblegum. 'I'll have plenty of time to finish off my sweets. I'll just stand by that door.'

I stared at Joe. How come he was suddenly so relaxed about not being on camera? I was about to find out.

'That's right. *Take your time* – enjoy,' laughed Amor, winking at Joe. 'I'm sure the Finns won't mind if you explore their *interesting* house . . .'

What? No way. What was going on? Stacey, Bill and I shot each other worried glances.

Amor pretended not to notice. Smiling blandly he said, to nobody in particular: 'What a nice boy Joe is. He reminds me so much of myself at that age . . . Now, Ned. Joe's warned me that you find understanding things difficult, so we've printed your answers on some big cue cards which the crew will hold up. If you prefer, you can also read them off this large screen called an autocue. Let's practise!'

So we did.

The script was terrible. Each answer was the same, except for the one about Joe Blagg which was so flattering about him that I choked. Whatever he was up to, I knew one thing: by the end of the show, the viewers would be bored rigid and I'd have the world's worst tummy ache having eaten the equivalent of one kilo of cabbage, two bags of prunes and a plateful of mixed veg.

But there was no time to complain. Everyone else was doing that already.

'It's like an oven in here,' wailed the cameraman (inserting an adjective which is definitely not allowed in our house), as he dabbed his forehead

129

with a filthy handkerchief. 'Where's the air conditioning? These lights are dreadful. For goodness' sake, Rodney! What are you up to?'

'OK, OK, keep your hair on,' growled Rodney, unplugging one cable from here, replugging it there, tripping over one of the ninety-seven cables on the floor with every move. 'Not that you have any, that is!'

The cameraman sulked but his reply – which included more forbidden adjectives – was drowned out by a deafening scream from the make-up lady. 'Ahhh! Look at that boy; he's as pasty as a mashed potato! Bring him to me!'

And before I knew what was happening, an alarming-looking lady with a large paintbrush started plastering my face with a vast range of creams, powders, eyeliner and lip gloss. 'Dear, dear, dear,' she muttered, 'what drab skin tone. Just as well I brought the emergency kit . . .'

After me it was Stacey's turn (she loved it – this woman's make-up box was even bigger than hers), followed by Bill, then Mum and Dad, who were pulled away from the back door where they'd been standing looking increasingly shell-shocked. The lady was just searching for Joe, when Amor Ron twirled about and clapped his hands. For a big man he was certainly pretty nimble.

'Right, everyone, positions please! We're about to go on air. Stacey, Bill, Mr and Mrs Finn, will you please go and stand over there by the table? Now, Ned, sit down and keep calm! Stacey, what are you doing in front of camera three? Raspberry boy – get out of my shot! Go back by the door. And where's Joe? . . . Oh, for goodness' sake, couldn't he have gone to the toilet before? Well, just make sure you put him close to the mike when he gets back. Now, take your places everyone and good luck!'

There was a sudden silence as the runner began her countdown:

'10 . . . 9 . . . 8 . . .'

I looked round nervously, but my mind was numb. Any second now and I would be live – live on national TV. Stacey rushed forward and hugged me.

'Get off!' I hissed. But Stacey wouldn't budge.

'I want to be a star!' she screamed, kicking her legs in the air as she was hauled off by three cameramen and dumped at the back of the room.

'7 . . . 6 . . . 5 . . .'

131

Mum and Dad waved cheerily as instructed. But I was as cheery as limp lettuce. Sweat was trickling down my spine and I could hear my costume making weird creaking sounds. The foliage felt like a noose. The room stank of boiled cabbage, stewed prunes and . . . hang on . . . *what was Dad up to?* I stared in horror as he suddenly produced a huge placard from behind his back saying: 'Buy Finn's *Finn-tastic* Fish Food!' and started waving it above Mum's head. Honestly, parents! If Amor saw it he'd throw a wobbly.

This was a disaster.

'4 . . . 3 . . .' recited the runner.

My heart started pounding in my ears and my throat felt dry. That trickle of sweat had turned into a torrent. Amor was mouthing, 'Where's Joe?' at the producer, who simply shrugged back.

Thump!

I knew exactly where Joe was – in my bedroom! And there could be only one reason for that.

Clang! Bash!

I pushed back my chair. Live show or no live show, I *had* to save Lucky. But how? There was a sudden flash of lights as the cameras began to whirr into action. 'Sit still!' hissed Amor, grabbing my arm. 'We're about to go live!'

As if on cue the runner called out: '2 . . . 1 . . . ACTION!' and a terrifying scream rent the air. It was Joe. In my bedroom.

'AGGGGH! Come quick! I've found a *monster!'*

Chapter 15
LIGHTS OUT!

As soon as I heard Joe's cry I started to panic. So did Stacey. Letting out a scream that she's perfected over years of practice on me, she charged towards the door, closely followed by Bill. Mum and Dad tried to follow, but they tripped over the make-up lady's tool box and crashed to the ground, scattering eyeshadow, brushes, blushers and foundations all over the floor.

'STAND STILL, all of you!' hissed the producer. 'We're LIVE!'

Back in front of the camera, Amor Ron did his best to pretend that nothing was wrong. Gritting his teeth, he presented me with a bowl of stewed prunes and fired off question number one.

'Well done, Ned, that film clip was fantastic! Inspiring. Even moving. Tell me, do you enjoy learning to swim?'

'Ooh, *nooo*!' Joe's anguished cry floated down from the room above.

Startled, Amor knocked over the bowl of prunes. I hardly noticed. I was too worried about Lucky. From the corner of my eye I could see Stacey and Bill trying to force their way to the door, blocked at every turn by the burly film crew.

Amor wiped his brow and fired off question number two.

'Ned, I understand that you are no longer the class idiot but are now top of the form! Do you think . . .' he paused, placing a plate of boiled cabbage in front of me with a flourish, 'this is because you are eating so many of my delicious fruit and vegetables?'

I wiggled my nose.

'*Yuck*!' hollered Joe from upstairs. '*This stuff stinks*!'

I blinked. Either Joe disliked the smell of boiled cabbage as much as me – or he'd just stepped in some dino poop.

'Well,' exclaimed Amor, his smile telling me exactly what he intended to do to me once the cameras had stopped rolling. 'Let's move on quickly to our last question. Tell me, Ned; has Joe Blagg, your school's Champion Swimmer, given you any useful tips about the Swimmathon?'

Silence.

Instinctively, we both looked up at the ceiling.

'Now, come on, Ned,' urged Amor, grinning at the cameras. 'Don't be shy . . .' adding in a voice only I could hear: *Just read the answer on the auto-cue!* So, tilting back my head to free it from the fake foliage, I did my best. Unfortunately, the leaves kept getting tangled up in my tongue, making me lisp.

'Fl-Joe,' I read out, 'if fleally –'

'HORRIBLE . . . TRULY, TRULY HORRIBLE!' yelled Joe at the top of his voice, thumping across the landing.

I coughed and tried again. Gritting my teeth, I took a deep breath.

'Fl-Joe's advice . . .' I read out, raising my voice, 'fl-was –'

'USELESS!'

'And,' I cried, almost screaming in panic, 'FW-EVERYONE FW-AT SCHOOL FW-INKS HE IS A –'

'DISGUSTING SMELLY SKUNK!'

The door flew open and there stood Joe, holding something in his hands. Something which was small and feathery with pink and purple spots and a pair of Stacey's pink frilly knickers balanced on its head . . .

'LUCKY!' cried Stacey in despair. 'Joe's caught Lucky! Quick, Ned, *DO* something. Save him!'

So I did. Pushing myself away from the table, I lunged forward to grab the dinosaur from our enemy, when . . . ping! My overheated tomato costume suddenly blew up like a balloon and sent me whizzing backwards across the floor. I landed on my back with a painful thud . . . right on top of the big yellow box with that bright red knob.

BANG!

The room was plunged into darkness.
Amor's live TV show was off the air.

Chapter 16
EGGS-CAPE!

As soon as the lights went out, there was a stunned silence and then everyone went mad — especially Amor Ron. 'What's going on?' he yelled as the crew screamed, shouted and rushed about, bumping into each other as they searched for torches, switches, fuses — anything to get the show back on air. 'Where are the emergency lights?' cried Amor. 'Where's Joe? What's happened to Ned? When I find out who's responsible for this, I'll *kill* them!'

Well, I know whose fault it was: Joe's.

But I knew who would get the blame: me. I made a quick plan:

1. Stacey, Bill and I were going to rescue Lucky.
2. We were going to leg it to the safest hiding place we could think of – which was quite difficult given that we were dressed up as a bright red (exploding) tomato, a carrot and a raspberry with baggy tights.
3. I was going to confess to everything, but only when I had escaped to a desert island that was totally lacking in:
   a) TV cameras
   b) Bullies
   c) Any way for any adult to possibly find me.

Until then I had to find a way of heaving myself up from the floor. At that moment I was floundering around with my legs in the air, flipping this way and that. The more I struggled, the more I became tangled up in wires and lamp stands. Finally, I found myself gripping the base of a sturdy pole. I hauled myself up with relief – only to discover it wasn't a pole, it was Terri the soundman's leg.

'Oi, what's going on?' he cried, grabbing my shoulder and helping me to my feet. 'Watch out or you'll knock over my boom!'

But it was too late. As he put out his hand to help me, the fluffy grey lollipop slipped forward. It ripped through a large white cue sheet and crashed down on the table in front of Amor Ron, tipping my plate of lukewarm cabbage straight into his lap.

'*Yow*,' he cried, pushing his chair (which was on castors) back on to Joe's foot.

'*Youch!*' howled Joe, letting go of Lucky and hopping up and down in pain.

'Yum!' squawked our pet, guzzling the vegetables. And even then he might have been all right had Mum not found the large and powerful emergency torch in the cupboard under the sink . . . and turned it on.

The effect was electric. In the torchlight, Lucky's shadow loomed huge and dark in a pool of light on the kitchen wall. Never a pretty sight, Lucky now looked like some vast and terrifying alien with bulging eyes, pulsating neck and sinister, evil grin.

The crew took one glimpse and screamed.

'*AAAAAAAAAAAAAAAAH*, it's a monster!' shouted a cameraman.

'. . . a kitten . . .' cried the make-up lady.

'. . . a ghost . . .' shrieked the chef.

'Here, gimme that torch,' snarled Amor, snatching it from Mum and waving it around. 'I want that creature! I don't care if it's the legendary yeti from Outer Peregulavia, it ruined my show!'

Arms, legs, chairs, tables, food and words flew back and forth as everyone tried to catch our prehistoric pet. Seizing our chance, Bill, Stacey and I bounced round the kitchen hunting for Lucky.

'Get off my toe!' cried Rodney as he bumped into the make-up lady.

'Leave that poor little kitten alone, you brute,' she replied, shaking a pot of powder over his head.

'Gimme that boom!' shouted Terri as he grabbed Dad's placard by mistake.

'FOOD FIGHT!' yelled Joe, lobbing a tomato at us. Dodging it neatly, we dropped to the floor.

'Where's Lucky?' wailed Stacey, wiggling through Terri the soundman's legs.

'I don't know,' I answered, ducking as a plate of stewed prunes hurtled through the air.

'On top of the counter,' cried Bill, as the producer strafed the room with Mum's torch only to be splattered with a dollop of custard. 'Quick, Lucky! Jump on to the pendant light!'

'Oh no you don't,' growled Joe, running forward. 'I found him, I'll keep him!'

'Well, you can't!' cried Stacey. 'Take this!' And seizing a large cue card, she rammed it over his head.

'Ouch,' Joe moaned as Lucky, clumsy as ever, used his enemy's face as a launch pad and jumped on to the light via his nose.

There was no time to lose. Bill and I grabbed the sound boom and thwacked it at the light, making it – and Lucky – swing crazily towards the window. There was the sound of broken glass and . . . silence. Our plucky little Lucky had escaped through the window, into the garden and was free.

But unfortunately, we were not. Where once Mr Amor Ron had oozed charm, he now spat poison.

'*Get out of my sight, you miserable bunch of grubby vegetables!*' he screamed. 'Do you realise how much money you've cost me? This show's a fiasco, a disaster, a financial flop! Now, Ned Finn, where are your parents? You're their son, so it's their fault. I want, no, *demand*, to speak to them. So scam, scoot, vamoose – *GET LOST!*'

I didn't need telling twice. Turning tail, I rushed

out of the kitchen quickly followed by Stacey, Bill . . .

and Joe.

'Come back here!' he yelled. 'I want a word with you.'

Well, he might, but we didn't. Given the situation, there was only one thing we could do:

RUN.

Hitching up our costumes, we legged it out of the garden and down the road. You can imagine how surprised the townsfolk were to see a tomato, a carrot and a raspberry running down the street – followed by a muscle-bound figure in a torn blue suit with a handful of beans in his hair. By the time we reached the end of the high street we were out of breath and fading fast. Sweat was pouring off us and the back of my thighs were rubbed raw by my costume. Stacey was limping and Bill's breath was coming in great ragged gasps. It was only a matter of time before we were caught.

'Stop, we must stop,' I wheezed as we turned a corner and found ourselves (temporarily) out of Joe's sight.

'Yes, yes,' panted Stacey. 'But where can we hide?'

'In here!' shouted Bill and, without waiting for

our reply, he dashed through the open doorway of the museum. The hall was dark and empty except for a stern-looking woman wearing a thick pair of horn-rimmed glasses. She was sitting at the information desk, busily sorting through a bundle of postcards.

'Good afternoon. Come to see the dinosaur exhibition, have you?' she said, without glancing up. 'It's up the stairs, first hall on the left, but mind! We close in fifteen minutes exactly!'

So not knowing what else to do, we went upstairs towards the exhibition. At first, Stacey hung back. 'I can't go in,' she wailed. 'What happens if someone sees us dressed like this?'

'Oh, don't worry,' soothed Bill. 'They'll probably just crack a joke!'

'Such as?' snarled Stacey, her eyes flashing.

'Well, you know: "*Why did the carrot go out with a prune?*"'

Stacey sniffed suspiciously. 'I don't know – why?'

'Because she couldn't get a date!'

'Now, come on you two, get serious,' I pleaded as Stacey tried to thump Bill. Honestly, couldn't those two stop winding each other up for just a moment? 'If we get –'

'. . . carrot-ed away,' crowed Bill, dodging as Stacey kicked him on the shins.

'. . . we'll *never* find Lucky. And who knows, we might learn something useful about him in the exhibition. It *is* about dinosaurs, after all.'

'Yes, of course, you're right,' agreed Stacey, suddenly full of concern. 'That poor little thing must be so scared. Do you . . . do you think we'll ever see him again?'

'Yes!' I replied. 'Look!'

And there was Lucky, crouched in front of a life-sized model of two fighting dinosaurs. He seemed mesmerised by their jerky mechanical movements, their glowing eyes, their computer-programmed roars and their scaly skin. When he heard our voices, instead of turning round and greeting us with a cheerful smile, he ducked his head and started to sob. Great tears rolled down his cheeks and his tiny hunched body looked as weak and vulnerable as a bird with a broken wing. We rushed over to him.

'Lucky, what's the matter? Don't be upset by these dinosaurs, they're only animatronic – pretend models!' I reassured him gently.

'Yes, and there's no need to panic about that

beastly Joe either. We'll sort him out,' consoled Bill as Stacey enveloped Lucky in a large and comforting, carroty hug.

'It's not Joe I'm upset about – although I can't believe I allowed myself to be captured by that half-wit – it's *that*!' And lifting his head, Lucky stared at the plastic models.

I was puzzled. True, the dinosaurs did look realistic. On the left was a Tyrannosaurus[31] rex, complete with a thick tail, two sturdy back legs, a massive neck and a pair of puny arms.

On the right, pinned to the ground by the T. rex's huge, three-toed foot was a smooth-skinned dinosaur with a long neck, bulging eyes, large tummy and tiny head. I peered at it closely. It was a very pale shade of pink, and when you looked carefully, you could see faded purple spots. There were definitely claws on its paws and its mouth was filled with hundreds of sharp, white teeth.

'Bill,' I whispered, 'what's this dinosaur called?'

But it was Lucky who answered my question.

'She's called a Plodothod,' he sobbed. 'And she's my mum.'

---

[31] *Tie-RAN-oh-sore-us*

Chapter 17
FOSSIL FINDS

'*Your mum?*' I repeated. 'Are . . . are you sure?'

Lucky nodded. 'I recognised her as soon as I came into the room. Look at the teeth . . . and the legs . . . and that tail. Oh, Stacey,' he sighed, gazing adoringly at the model dinosaur, 'you were *so* right. I'm as lucky as my name. She's *beautiful.*'

We stared at Lucky; then we stared at his mum. Beautiful was not quite the adjective I'd have chosen to describe a large tubby crested creature with a tiny toothy head and a neck as long as a giraffe's. But then, everyone loves their mum. And when I studied the model more closely there could be no doubt; Lucky *was* a Plodothod.

'But this is wonderful!' cried Bill. 'Plodothods were really rare! I don't think even Professor Bron T. Saurus lists you in his book. Hey, listen to this information sheet:

THE PLODOTHOD

*This dinosaur was the
stupidest, smelliest, slowest,*

*greediest and laziest
creature ever to have walked on the face of this earth. It
lived over sixty-five million years ago
and was VERY RARE.
Experts think this is because
IT WAS TOO LAZY TO HATCH ITS OWN
EGGS!*

'*Lazy? Me? Stupid? Me? Greedy? Me?*' shouted Lucky, jumping out of Stacey's arms. 'I'm the brightest thing on four legs, a dinosaur of distinction! I have style, flair, brains! I can speak two hundred languages, practise yoga, mimic voices *and* do tongue twisters. I can even say MICROPACHYCEPHALOSAURUS . . .'

'. . . *Mike-row-pak-ee-keff-ah-loh-sore-us, a tiny thick-headed plant-eating lizard . . .*' whispered Bill helpfully.

'. . . and METRIACANTHOSAURUS . . .'

'. . . *Met-ree-a-kan-tho-sore-us, a carnivorous lizard from the Jurassic Period . . .*'

'. . . without pausing for breath!' finished Lucky indignantly.

'OK, OK,' I said, hastily smoothing Lucky's ruffled feathers. 'They've obviously made a mistake.

What else does it say, Bill?'

'Well . . .' Bill shifted uncomfortably from foot to foot:

No one knows EXACTLY what this dinosaur looked like – except that it was VERY, VERY FAT! But that's not surprising! From the remains of a HUGE dino poo, we know that this greedy guzzler ate everything it could: vegetables, fish, meat, stones, trees, sand . . . anything, in fact, that was lying around.

Lucky was furious. Unfortunately, the next section was no better.

TRUE OR FALSE?

Spookily, some people believe that the Plodothod is
THE LOCH NESS MONSTER
(or 'Nessie' for short!)
Eyewitnesses claim to have seen a creature that looks just like the Plodothod living in a great lake called Loch Ness in Scotland. No one has ever found it – but then, there are plenty of places for it to hide! Let us know if you see one!

152

There was a stunned silence.

'*The Loch Ness Monster?*' howled Lucky. 'I'm not a *monster*. I'm a dinosaur – a Plodothod. Pray tell me, who, or what, is this Nessie?'

I swallowed hard. This was going to take some explaining. 'The Loch Ness Monster, Lucky, is a legend – a myth, a mystery! It's only called a monster because it's so huge. Some people swear that they have seen –'

'. . . a great prehistoric creature with a long neck, small head . . . ' interrupted Stacey.

'. . . large humps and a pointy tail . . .' added Bill.

'. . . swimming in the loch,' I finished. 'There have been loads of photographs taken,' I continued, adding quickly, 'Many sightings are considered to have been fakes. Scientists have spent *a fortune* trying to prove that you exist!'

'Yes – and you do! Isn't that brilliant?' laughed Stacey. 'For now we know what you are and where you live. All that's left is for us to find someone to take you back home – to Loch Ness!'

'But . . . *who?*' asked Lucky, almost jumping up and down with excitement.

'Well, that's easy,' chuckled Bill. 'Ned! I have the perfect plan.' And he was just about to tell us all

153

when we heard a terrible cry from the lady with the horn-rimmed glasses, followed by the sound of Joe's footsteps pounding up the stairs.

Chapter 18
TONGUE TWISTERS

'Quick, Lucky, hide in my costume!' I gasped.

'No, thank you, Ned,' said the dinosaur. 'It's time someone taught that primate a lesson!' And he scrambled up the back of the model T. rex and concealed himself in its gaping plastic mouth.

Joe burst into the hall. 'Right,' he snarled, advancing towards us menacingly. 'Where is *it*? Where's that mutant guinea pig?'

'HERE!' moaned a strange and sinister voice.

Joe jumped.

'OK, Ned,' he said, thrusting his big bulgy nose in my face. 'So you're a ventriloquist, are you? Well, watch my lips! I suggest you find me that alien right now! Otherwise, as well as speaking without moving your mouth, you'll be speaking without using your brain!' Joe pulled back his arm as if to hit me. I winced. I could see every one of the black spots on his nose and smell every sweet he'd devoured during the show.

'Joeee, oh, Joeee,' called the Voice. 'I'm over heeeeere. Why don't you come and find me?'

'Agggh!' Flustered, Joe ran round the room as Lucky chanted the following tongue twister increasingly fast: '*Red lorry, yellow lorry, red lorry,*

yellow lorry.' Finally Joe came to a rest beside Stacey, who kept her mouth firmly shut.

'Hah,' crowed Lucky, clearly enjoying himself. 'Are you still confused? Did you think I was Stacey? Well, watch her lips and listen to this:

Peter Piper picked a peck of pickled peppers.
Did Peter Piper pick a peck of pickled peppers?
If Peter Piper picked a peck of pickled peppers,
Where's the peck of pickled peppers Peter Piper picked?

Aren't I clever?' chortled Lucky immodestly. 'It's taken me *days* to learn that one. Bet you couldn't manage that once without a mistake!'

'Huh – but *I'm* not mistaken about you,' snarled Joe. 'If it's not Stacey's voice, it must be Bill's!' And he grabbed my brother by the scruff of his raspberry costume's neck. But like Stacey, Bill kept his mouth firmly shut as Lucky sang out the following words:

She sells seashells by the seashore.
The shells she sells are surely seashells
So if she sells shells on the seashore
I'm sure she sells seashore shells!

157

It was all too much. Joe spun round and glowered at us all. 'OK,' he shouted. 'If it isn't Bill, or Ned, or Stacey . . . *who is it?*'

'MEEEEEEEEEE!' growled the T. rex in a low and angry voice. 'The ghost of Dinosaurs Past!'

'Ghost!' scoffed Joe, striding up to the dinosaur. 'You're not a ghost – just a plastic mock-up of a has-been monster!' He peered angrily at the model. 'Whoever's hiding in there, come out and face me *at once!*'

'Are you sure? Be afraid . . . Be *very* afraid . . . ! It's very dangerous to disturb a ghoooooost.'

'I'll take my chance! You . . . you *dummy!*' spat Joe, clenching his fists.

The Tyrannosaurus[32] began to move. Its head started tilting towards Joe. Down and down it came until it was just within reach of the bully and then . . .

It let out the loudest cry I have ever heard.

So did Joe. 'AAaaaah, help!' he cried, as he took to his heels and plunged down the staircase.

'For goodness' sake, can't you look where you're going?' cried the woman with the horn-rimmed glasses. 'It's closing time. Are the others still up there?' But Joe didn't stop to answer. Nor did we.

[32] *Tie-RAN-oh-sore-us*

'Quick,' I shouted, grabbing Lucky from the mouth of the Tyrannosaurus[33] rex and stuffing him into the hollow of my costume. 'Let's go before we get into more trouble!'

And together we rushed out of the exhibition hall, down the fire escape and back into the fresh air.

'Phew,' gasped Stacey. 'We made it, we're free!'

'Yes, thanks to Lucky!' smiled Bill as he struggled to catch his breath.

'Oh, it was nothing!' laughed Lucky, popping his head out of my costume. 'I simply used the microphone and hotwired the technology in the Tyrannosaurus's[34] mouth to make it move. It's simple really, as long as you know how.'

'Well, let's hope it's as simple to get ourselves out of the next mess,' I muttered. And ignoring the rude looks and sniggers of passers-by, we made our way back home. We were all exhausted; we were all looking forward to a little peace and quiet.

But unfortunately, that was the last thing we found.

---

[33] *Tie-RAN-oh-sore-us*
[34] *Tie-RAN-oh-sore-us-ez*

Chapter 19
AMOR HATCHES
A PLAN

When we reached home, the house was still in uproar.

Mum and Dad were rushing round making cups of tea, the crew was packing up its equipment, whilst outside the back door, Amor Ron was yelling down his mobile phone.

'Uh oh,' said Stacey, edging away from the garden gate. 'Do you . . . do you think we should go in?'

'No, let's come back when everyone's calmer,' I agreed.

'Yeah, in about a hundred zillion years,' muttered Bill.

'Oh, cheer up,' whispered Lucky. 'It might not be as bad as you think!'

Just then Joe burst out of the kitchen door.

'I quit,' he shouted at Amor Ron. 'Those Finns are mad! I don't care about the race. I'm *not* Ned's Buddy and I'm *not* going to swim with that bozo ever again. I'm through!'

Amor Ron instantly snapped off his phone. 'Joe, Joe, *Joe* . . .' he soothed, 'relax! You and Ned are comic geniuses. Your stunt was *brilliant*! Since going off the air, customers have been queuing up everywhere to buy my fruit and vegetables. Sales are rocketing. You've made me a mint of money. And Joe,' he continued in a completely different voice, 'I know how to make a mint more — *if* you will help me! Come this way!'

And with a furtive look over his shoulder he slipped behind Mum and Dad's makeshift shelter that was shielding the garden.

Joe hesitated and followed.

And so, at a discreet distance, did we. Crouching behind a huge turnip, we strained our ears to overhear their conversation.

'What's all the fuss about?' asked Joe, pushing a potato leaf out of his face. 'There's nothing here but

a dirty great bunch of fruit and veg.'

'Wrong, Joe!' corrected Amor gleefully. 'Dirty, great *profitable* fruit and veg! Why, this rhubarb's as tall as you and those lettuce leaves are like a mini-forest. No wonder Mr and Mrs Finn were trying to hide them from me. I thought they were only interested in fish, but now I know better. These plants are worth their weight in gold. If I can find the root – *ha, ha* – of their success and steal it, I shall be able to create the biggest fruit and vegetable empire the world has ever seen. I shall be rich, Joe, rich beyond my wildest dreams. And believe you me, when it comes to money, my dreams aren't just wild, they're *CRAZY*. Which is why,' he added, holding out a handful of earth, 'I'm so glad I know what their secret is: *Dino dung!*'

We gasped. So did Joe. '*Euuch*,' he squealed, 'those look just like the stinky pellets I found in Ned's socks. What are they doing out here?'

'Because Ned's pet – the one you've been looking for with my help, the one you found in his cupboard – is a dinosaur!'

'*A dinosaur?*' repeated Joe. 'Are . . . are you sure?'

'Completely,' cried Amor. 'You see, Joe,' continued the businessman, mopping his brow, 'I know a *lot* about dinosaurs. I was once the star pupil of that great dino expert, Professor Bron T. Saurus. Have you heard of him? No? Pity. It was because of him that I discovered an amazing valley in Siberia. Ah . . . those were the days . . .' And before Joe knew what was happening, Amor took a deep breath and began to detail the look, size, colour, intelligence, hearing and feeding habits of every dinosaur known to man and then compared and contrasted them to and with the rival merits of Pterodactyls[35], Tyrannosauruses[36], Diplodocuses[37] and amoebas, rainfalls, climate change, big bangs and whatever other ideas he could think of. And guess what? He was *EVEN DULLER THAN BILL*. I couldn't help sympathising with Joe as he scratched his nose, yawned and shuffled his feet. Bill, on the other hand, was riveted. I had just decided that watching paint dry would be more interesting than listening to Amor bore on for one more moment when the villain said something that jerked me wide awake.

'And so that was when I discovered the reason for these outstanding crop yields: prehistoric poop! That valley was knee-deep in it. I only had to stick a seed or bulb into the earth and whoosh! Up it popped, rain or shine, summer or winter, within days of being planted. Well, I spent every last penny buying that glen, but then disaster struck. There was a terrible flood. The valley was drowned under thirty metres of water! Since then, I have searched the world for that same soil – and here it is, in Cattlebury!'

'But if that creature *is* a dinosaur, why didn't the

[35] TERRO-*dak-tils*
[36] *Tie-RAN-oh-sore-us-ez*
[37] *DI-plod-oh-kuss-ez*

Finns take it to the police?' objected Joe.

'Because Dan Finn's an idiot, a manufacturing muppet!' sneered Amor. 'He genuinely believes that the creature he saw in the kitchen this afternoon was part of a publicity stunt – keeps going on and on about it. But Ned – that boy's different. If he's guessed the truth, he'll try to keep that dinosaur a secret. Which is where you come in: Joe, I want you to filch Finn's fossil!'

'But . . . but aren't dinosaurs a bit dangerous?' protested Joe, spotting an obvious flaw.

'Detail, Joe, mere detail. We'll cage it up on a remote island. You can look after it. I promise you, there'll be no school – and just think of the sweets you could buy with the money!'

Joe's eyes lit up. 'But what would we feed it on?'

'Oooph!' replied Amor Ron carelessly. 'Anyone we didn't like. Heads of state . . .'

'Ned Finn . . .'

'Taxmen . . .'

'Stacey Finn . . .'

'Traffic wardens . . .'

'Bill Finn . . .'

'Unaccompanied violinists . . . bagpipe players . . . Morris dancers . . . but then,' sighed Amor, 'I

suppose the dinosaur might be a vegetarian. Oh well, we can't have everything – *though I like to try!* At least we'll be able to feed it for free. So, Joe: will you help me steal that dinosaur? Will you find it, catch it and bring it back to me? Mind, it's a secret. No one else must know!'

'No worries,' cried Joe. 'It'll be like taking candy from a baby. You see, Mr Ron, I wanna be rich! I want revenge on Ned Finn! I'll steal the school's stinky swimming skunk – just you wait!'

167

Chapter 20
THE LOCH NESS EGGS-PERIENCE

It was the worst week of my life.

Ever.

Following his decision to kidnap Lucky, life with Joe became a game of cat and mouse. Joe spent all his time rifling through my bags, spying on me with binoculars or glowering at me over school lunch.

'Where is it?' he'd growl as he chased me in the pool during one of our filming sessions.

'Give it to me!' he'd

yell as he tripped me up in the playground.

Of course, even under threat, Bill never lost an opportunity to bang on about dinosaurs. 'Wow, this is like the American Bone Wars between those two dino experts, Marsh and Cope,' gasped Bill as we holed up in the art room during break. 'They chased each other all over America in the nineteenth century trying to find and nick each other's fossils!'

He had a point. Joe was so keen to get his hands on my skin that I'd soon be reduced to a skeleton. And the journalists were just as bad – pursuing me everywhere to glean each detail of my keep-fit routine. It was so exhausting I nearly hid in the library and started my school project. But what else could I do? You see, when it comes to bullies, I follow the rules:

If you are being bullied
1. TELL AN ADULT
2. AVOID BEING ON YOUR OWN
WITH THE BULLY
3. DON'T FIGHT BACK

But I couldn't tell an adult because that might mean endangering Lucky; I couldn't avoid Joe because he was my swimming buddy; and as for not fighting, well, Joe was bigger . . . and fitter . . . and meaner. But we had one advantage: Lucky was smellier. Whenever Joe came too close, Lucky would (and excuse me if this shocks you) *whiff* so badly that Joe would swim or run in the other direction. Even Mum and Dad noticed the smell.

'Now, Ned,' comforted Mum one evening, holding a handkerchief to her nose, 'you must try not to be so anxious. Your tummy seems to be tying itself in knots. Don't let all the fuss upset you so much − your interviews have been brilliant and Amor tells me the Swimmathon is turning into a huge success. Hundreds of people are going to come and watch you at Loch Ness as well as TV crews and the media. Mr Peaseby's so excited that he's even asked me to knit a whole load of midge hats in the school colours. Look!' And she handed me a rectangular knitted tube. It reminded me of Dad's balaclava, except that it had a clear plastic visor to see through.

'Apparently,' added Mum excitedly, 'the loch is thick with those tiny insects and they have a nasty bite. We're going to sell the hats to raise money for the school library. Although,' she sighed, 'I can't

help wishing that the colours were a little less . . . startling.' I sympathised. There wasn't a pupil yet who'd looked good in our uniform of acid-yellow and purple.

As for Dad, he was fizzing round the house like a rocket about to lift off. 'Why, Tadpole,' he boomed, dragging out his fishing tackle from the cupboard under the stairs, 'this trip is just what I need! It's time for me to stop floundering around and carping on about my failures. I have to seize the fish by the Finn, salmon up my courage and trawl my way through deep water until I *Finn*-ally come up with some *Finn*-tastic ideas that will help me create the world's *Finn*-est fish food. Just imagine,' he breathed, gripping me tightly on the shoulder with one hand whilst stretching out the other as though towards a vision, 'you, me and my fish crisps, standing side by side on the podium being cheered to the skies; *you* for winning the Swimmathon, and *me* for saving the fish stocks of the world . . .'

'Oh, Dan,' breathed Mum, clasping her hands together. 'What a wonderful thought!'

And what a dreadful journey. Despite all Mum and Dad's promises, the drive up to Scotland at the end of term was far from fun.

'Why do I have to sit in the middle seat just because I'm the smallest? It's *so unfair!*' whined Bill.

'Tell Ned to stop breathing my air,' snarled Stacey.

'I'm going to be sick,' I moaned (well, so would you if you'd secretly chain-eaten as many sweets as me).

As for Lucky . . . I have to admit, our plucky little Plodothod did not make the ideal travelling companion. And why?

1. He smelt
2. He snored
3. When awake he <u>never</u> stopped talking to Bill and Stacey about . . .
   Dinosaurs.

Each time he spoke, he mimicked one of our voices so that Mum and Dad didn't become suspicious. It must have been exhausting for him. I know my head ached from listening to him – and trying to avoid Mum and Dad cottoning on.

'Could dinosaurs fly?' (Bill's question to Lucky)

'Flies?' (Mum) 'No, I'm knitting *midge* hats . . .'

'What noise did they make?' (Stacey)

'Noise? That's the gearbox . . .' (Dad)

'Are we there yet?' (Me, attempting to smooth things over)

'NO!' (Everyone)

'Well, can we stop? I need to go to the loo . . .' (I didn't, but I had to find some peace and quiet . . .)

Fortunately neither Mum nor Dad realised they had a hitch-hiker in the car. Dad was too busy driving and Mum (who was supposed to be map-reading) was so distracted by her knitting that it was no wonder we appeared to be taking the longest and most tortuous route to Loch Ness ever. (I know, I know. *You* may have sat nav, but then you might also have a car that doesn't start with a cranking handle . . .)

And then, just as I thought that my prayers had been answered and:

a) Lucky might have lost the power of speech
or
b) Bill and Stacey might have run out of questions,

Dad began to behave in the oddest way possible – even for him. Hunched over the steering wheel, he kept looking nervously from left to right and checking the mirror as if to see if we were being followed. As soon as he could, he turned off the main road and drove the car up a bumpy, rutted farm track, bringing it to a halt behind a gate at the edge of a field.

'Sssh!' hushed Dad loudly, putting his fingers to his mouth. Switching the radio on full blast, he opened the sunroof and peered out with a pair of binoculars he always keeps in the glove compartment. Then he closed the hatch and shut all the windows. Stacey rolled her eyes. Dad scuttled round to the boot of the car. A few seconds later he returned, carrying an old blanket covered in dog hairs. 'Quick, everyone,' he ordered, clambering back inside the car and lifting the rug over his head. 'Hide under this!'

Bill nudged me in the ribs and tried hard not to giggle. But I suddenly started to feel anxious. Dad might be an eccentric inventor, with a tendency to talk in fish puns, but he's nobody's fool and his eyes were full of determination. So we draped the manky rug over our heads. Stacey sneezed. In the background, the sound of the music grew louder and louder. Dad ignored it. Finally, he switched on a torch, leant forward and said firmly, 'Now,

Plankton, you might have noticed that there's a bit of a smell in this car. Don't worry; I know just what it is . . .Bill, empty your pockets!'

Bill gasped. Under the blanket I could feel someone trembling. I thought it was Stacey, but then I realised it was me.

'But . . . but why . . . why, Dad?' Bill stalled.

'Because, son, I think it's high time that you introduced Mum and me to its contents. We want to meet . . . your dinosaur!'

Chapter 21
EGGS-POSED!

It was a huge relief. We told Mum and Dad everything – and this time, not only did they listen, they believed us!

'But how did you know that Lucky was hiding in my pocket?' asked Bill as the dinosaur sheepishly clambered on to Dad's lap.

'Well . . . there's been a lot of chat in the car today – and sometimes I cod-n't quite recognise all the voices! I thought I was herring things!' chuckled Dad, stroking Lucky's crest. 'You're a brilliant mimic, Lucky, but when you get excited, you forget to imitate the others and speak in your

177

own voice. But to be honest, I've been suspicious for a while. You see, Lucky, your egg was found by my great-grandfather Albert. He was a famous nineteenth-century fossil hunter who spent years searching for relics in America whilst playing the world's worst golf . . .'

Bill nudged me. 'But I thought *Dad* was the world's worst golfer?' he whispered.

'Maybe it runs in the family,' I replied, remembering how Dad had taken three-and-a-half hours to complete the crazy golf course for the Under-Tens the week before.

'Well,' continued Dad, ignoring us, 'the egg's been passed down from generation to generation hidden in his original golf bag on condition that, if it hatched, we were to do everything we could to protect it. On no account were we to hand it over to a zoo or the authorities. Well, the years passed and to be honest, I forgot all about its eggs-istence. At first, I truly thought Ned's dinosaur was an imaginary friend – especially as we never saw him. But when the food started disappearing, Mum's plants grew so big and you all became dino-mad, I suddenly put two and two together and hit upon the answer!'

'We're really proud of you,' added Mum. 'You've told us the truth all along. And you're quite right to want to release Lucky back into the wild! But Lucky, are you sure you want to live in Loch Ness? You might be very lonely up there on your own.'

'Don't worry,' he laughed. 'I'll be fine – though I shall miss your fish crisps, Mr Finn, not to mention Ned's socks! And besides, how could you hide me when I'm fully grown? Call it instinct, but I believe Loch Ness is my true home.'

And Lucky was so happy when he saw Loch Ness

that it was hard to disagree. As Dad drove along the side of the loch, Lucky poked his nose out of the window and breathed in a lungful of air. 'Hmm,' he sighed contentedly, 'just smell that water . . . and feel that fresh Highland breeze. Isn't it fantastic?'

It was. That afternoon, the great Loch Ness lay as calm and beautiful as a millpond. Its high rocky sides were covered in heather and yellow gorse. The view from the hotel was stunning. For once, the Finn family was speechless.

Until Joe and Amor arrived. The hotel was packed with spectators and school friends, organisers and TV crews, but that didn't stop our enemies from watching our every move. Fortunately, Mum and Dad had a plan.

'Hmm, Ned,' said Mum, spotting Amor spying on me from two holes cut out from his newspaper that he was reading upside-down in the hotel lounge, 'Why don't you go and change into your tomato suit? In fact, Dad and I think you should wear it all the time you're here. No one will mind – after all, you are the mascot. And if Lucky hides in that secret panel he'll be out of harm's way!'

'Good idea,' agreed Dad, 'especially as I've just found Joe skulking outside your door behind a pot plant. He'll be suspicious, but there's little he can do whilst we're around!'

Wearing a tomato suit in an hotel is as embarrassing as watching Dad dance. As I could not sit down, I ate my dinner lounging against the wall. Stacey passed me my food – which was fine except that she tended to nibble the nicer bits along the way. Of course, the hotel residents knew I was the mascot and treated the whole thing as a big joke. 'Why did the tomato blush?' teased one of them when I first entered the dining room.

'Because it saw the salad dressing!' answered another.

See what I mean?

But Joe's jibes were the pits. 'How do you fix a broken tomato, Ned? *With tomato paste!*' he'd cry as soon as he had an audience, whilst Amor would say, 'Don't get saucy with me, Ned! I only want the ketchup!'

Lucky, on the other hand, was full of enthusiasm. 'Oooph,' he sighed, clambering out from my tomato costume in the bedroom that evening, 'I can't wait for our swim tomorrow. I know it's silly, but I swear I keep hearing voices in my head calling me towards the water. Must be the excitement . . .' He nuzzled me gently under the chin as he thoughtfully chewed my sock. 'What time does the race start? 1 p.m? Great, that's 16 hours, 59 minutes to go! Don't fret Ned, I won't let you down, I *promise.*'

But he did. That night, when I went to tuck him up, Lucky had disappeared. He was not in his normal hiding place. Nor was he in the suitcases, the shower, behind the TV or eating the contents of the mini-bar.

'But where is he?' wailed Stacey, helping Bill sort

through the contents of my underwear drawer for the umpteenth time. 'Do you think he's been stolen by Amor and Joe?'

'No,' replied Mum firmly, peeking through a crack in the door. 'Otherwise why would they be spying on us from behind a tea trolley in the corridor?'

'Well, in that case,' growled Dad, 'let's split up and go and search the shore. It's still twilight and I've some strong torches in the car. If we're with you, Plankton, you won't be bothered by those morons.'

But though we searched and searched none of us could find sight nor sound of our pet. Straining my eyes, I stared out at the loch, trying to work out if that flashing dark shadow under the water was Lucky or a trick of the light. Dread clutched my stomach. Shivering with fear, I took a deep breath and plucked Dad's sleeve.

'Dad, do . . . do you think Lucky might have gone swimming in the loch and . . . *shrunk and shrunk and shrunk* . . . until he . . . *disappeared*?'

Dad clenched his jaw. 'I don't know, Tadpole. I really don't. We'll just have to wait and see.'

Chapter 22
THE BIG RACE

It was the morning of the race: the media event of the summer.

Despite all my prayers, there had been no drought, rock fall, cyclone, typhoon, mud slide, erupting volcano or flood. Instead the conditions were near perfect. The sun was shining and there was hardly a cloud (though plenty of midges) in the sky.

And absolutely no sign of Lucky.

By 12.30 p.m. I was feeling as sick as a dog – trembling on the edge of the shore in my battered red tomato suit, my stick-like arms and legs poking out of it like green twigs. Everywhere I looked contestants were bustling about – giving interviews, being photographed, asking questions and nervously laughing at jokes. A band played and the shore was crowded with spectators, school friends and TV crews, all jostling together happily, wearing Mum's brightly coloured midge hats – and reeking of cheap scent.

'Good luck, Ned!' shouted Mr Peaseby. 'Thanks for the midge hat, Mrs Finn. It's brilliant, particularly when I took your advice and sprayed it with my aftershave, *Cool Dude*. It works so well, I told everyone to do the same!' The head teacher was a sight to be seen in a yellow knitted midge hat, royal-blue blazer, emerald cycling shorts and a medallion that was nestling on his puny hair-free chest. He was puffing up and down the start line like an energetic steam engine, waving clipboards, posing for photographs – and telling anyone who would listen to him that he'd just seen the Loch Ness Monster.

'It was probably just his reflection,' whispered Stacey, trying to cheer me up. But I was too upset to laugh. Where was Lucky? I thought miserably. Was he safe? Was he alive? As for the race, we all knew the truth: without Lucky acting as my

personal onboard turbo-charged motor, I was sunk. Come 1 p.m., I would be revealed as a cheat and a fraud.

In public.

On national TV.

But I didn't care. I only cared about finding our dinosaur.

Suddenly, there was a spluttering noise and Amor Ron's voice floated towards me over the microphone.

'Ladies and gentlemen, boys and girls,' said the

businessman, looking like a yellow jelly bean in canary-yellow shorts and matching T-shirt. 'Welcome to the Loch Ness School Swimmathon. As many of you will know, at the start of this term, Ned Finn was voted – *unanimously* – the worst swimmer in the country. He couldn't swim at all. Now – thanks to my super vegetables and fruit, a sackload of which he eats EVERY WEEK – Ned is a water baby, a champion swimmer who is ABOUT TO START THE RACE! And how can you become as successful as Ned Finn? Well, all you have to do . . . as I am sure we can say together, is:

Be Bright!
Eat Right!
Buy Ron's Fruit and Veg Tonight!'

There was a huge cheer as the crowd chanted Amor Ron's slogan.

'Ha, if only they knew the truth!' sneered a voice behind me. I jumped. Dressed in a black wetsuit, Joe loomed above me like a sleek and evil shark. 'Make the most of your five minutes of fame, pond weed. I suppose . . .' he prodded my costume, 'that if you have to make a complete idiot of yourself, you might as well go out with a splash – *ha, ha*. But remember, if I don't get that dinosaur at the end of the race, you're dead meat!' And he slashed his finger across his neck and uttered a hollow and sinister laugh.

I blanched. Joe had grabbed my arm in a vice-like grip and was about to make another vile threat when Amor Ron's miked-up voice boomed once more across the shore.

'POSITIONS, PLEASE! Will the swimmers please make their way down to the starting line. Each contestant is to swim to the boat and then back to the shore. Well, ALL EXCEPT my mascot NED FINN. He simply has to swim twenty metres to that raft in order to start the race. Let's hope he isn't caught by the Loch Ness Monster!'

The crowd tittered.

I gulped.

This was it. And there was *still* no sign of Lucky.

'Right, off you go, Ned! Good luck!' said Amor Ron, running up and giving me a sharp push towards the loch. 'And don't forget,' he added with a menacing wink, 'I want that dinosaur. If you don't give it to me at the end of the race – WATCH OUT! I'll ruin you *and* your family. I'll sack Mr

Peaseby, close down Brackenbridge School and make sure you, Stacey and Bill are banned from every school in the country. Do I make myself clear?'

I nodded.

Trembling with nerves, I waddled down to the water's edge. There were twenty-seven swimmers taking part in the race and I could feel all their fifty-four eyes on my back. To my left was Red Rider, a great hulking fourteen-year-old boy with rippling muscles and a clean-cut jaw. To my right, a year younger, was the Elf, a girl with the shape of a whippet and a gaze that could freeze water into ice. And beyond her, laughing and making a thumbs-down sign . . . was Joe.

Gritting my teeth, I put my toe in the loch – and instantly jumped back. Even in my wetsuit that water was freezing. I tried again. But it was no good. Without Lucky I was lost.

'Come on, slowcoach, get going,' shouted one onlooker.

'Yeah, I thought you could swim!' jeered another.

I gazed round anxiously. Stacey and Bill were grinning madly and frantically making the thumbs-up sign to me. Mum and Dad watched with

agonised faces. Mr Peaseby had lost the plot completely and was kneeling on the shore, praying loudly for me to take the plunge. Only Amor, fishing net in one hand, kept calm, scanning the water with his powerful binoculars for a sign of Lucky. The puzzled and disappointed spectators were getting restless, whispering and pointing and wondering what was wrong.

There was nothing else for it: I had to move. Taking a deep breath, I stepped into the water. That was my left foot . . . Phew, it was cold, even in my suit.

Right calf . . . I had to keep going . . .

Left knee . . . could I do it? Could I? . . .

BANG!

A shattering noise cracked the air. Everyone jumped as Amor Ron seized a starting pistol from an official and started the race.

'NED FINN!' he yelled at me as the twenty-seven competitors raced fearlessly into the loch. 'The race has started without you. But you're *still* my mascot! Get into that water and swim or you're a –'

'Brilliant friend and swimmer!' said an unfamiliar and distinctly American voice from somewhere beneath the water. 'Come on, kiddo,' it encouraged, 'it's time to go! Let's show that old windbag how it's done!' And before I knew what was happening, I felt myself being lifted off my feet and thrust – at top speed – across the surface of the loch.

'But who . . . what are you? I don't understand!' I spluttered, frantically clinging on to the creature's thick and scaly tail.

'Oh, don't worry about that now, just swim!' laughed the mystery voice. 'Enjoy! Let me do all the hard work. Now hang on! We're off!'

And so we were. But to where? I thought as I clung on for grim death.

And with whom?

Chapter 23
MONSTER FUN

It was the best swim of my life.

Streaming through the water, I surged along in the wake of this unknown creature. Its hard scaly tail was covered in a series of rounded spikes so it was easy to hold on. In next to no time, we had reached the raft and the first set of safety boats. Thanks to my unknown friend, I'd swum my twenty metres, dodged Joe *and* saved my reputation and that of the school's. I was still dead worried about Lucky, but as far as I was concerned it was time for a well-earned rest.

'Stop, please stop,' I spluttered. 'This is as far as we

need to go!'

'What, that piddly wooden raft? Oh no, I think we can do better than that! *Especially* as I can see Mr Loud Mouth – that idiot Amor Ron – standing there with a large fishing net. I think he might be after me, don't you?'

'So what shall we do?' I panted.

'Swim faster!' chuckled the creature. And with that we struck out for deep water, following the other competitors who were way ahead of us.

One . . . two . . . three . . . we passed.

Then five . . .

Then eleven . . .

Then twenty . . .

I swam on until I suddenly realised that there were only three swimmers left in front: Red Rider, the Elf and . . . Joe.

To give him his due, Red Rider fought hard. His even strokes sliced through the water like a hot knife through butter. But he was no match for my mysterious friend. 'Way to go,' he yelled encouragingly as I pulled past. Unfortunately, the Elf was not so gracious. She tried every stroke she knew to stay ahead: crawl, backstroke, butterfly, breaststroke. But nothing worked. However much

she dipped, dived, turned and somersaulted, my companion stretched out his lead.

'Pah,' sulked the defeated girl, 'I'll never eat another stinky tomato again!'

'Don't worry, she'll get over it,' chortled my new swimming buddy. 'How do you feel? Shall we try and overtake Joe?'

'You bet!'

'Well, in that case, I'll need you to be brave and put your face in the water. That way we'll go faster. Tell you what; let's get some help from the crowd!' And then the creature shouted out in clear and ringing tones: 'COME ON, NED! COME ON, NED! COME ON, NED!'

The crowd went mad. Laughing, they started to chant, clap and stamp their feet to the rhythm. It was just what I needed. Taking a deep breath, I plunged my face into the water of my own free will for the first time in my life.

The shock of the icy water hit me like an explosion. I spluttered and choked as water filled my mouth, stung my eyes and gummed up my ears. Snorting and blowing, I gasped as I tried to rid it from my nose – but still I persevered. I wasn't going to let my friend down.

And then the most unexpected thing happened.

I started to relax.

Instead of swallowing mouthfuls of water, I began to breathe and turn my head just as Lucky had instructed me all those weeks ago on the bedroom stool. Breathe, two three. Breathe, two three. And the more I relaxed, the easier it became – and the faster we swam. If that is swimming, I thought, I'd love to be a fish!

Looking up briefly, I could see the finishing line straight ahead of us – just in front of Joe.

'Do you think we'll catch him up?' I gasped.

'Yup, if we hold our nerve! That bully might be a great swimmer, but he deserves to be taught a lesson. Otherwise, he'll turn everyone's life into a misery. Oh, by the way, you're doing great! Let's give it one more go!'

And we did.

We swam another metre . . . then another *and* another. We were just about to catch him up, when, 'Fluuuuuuuuuurrrrrrrp!'

My tomato costume began to dissolve, deflating rather like a week-old balloon. First I lost the armholes, then the green ruff and lastly the zip before it finally fell apart in a soggy mess. 'Help, STOP!' I choked, thrashing the water wildly with my arms. 'I'm drowning!'

'Nonsense,' chortled my unknown ally. 'Haven't you noticed how you've been swimming by yourself since you put your face in the water? I've just been keeping you company. Now relax and kick those legs. If you overtake Joe then you'll know not only that you can swim – but that you can swim really well!'

He was right. I sped past the bully and then, bruised, battered but buzzing with glee, I crossed the finish line and discovered that . . .

YES!!
I HAD WON!!!
I,
NED FINN . . .
COULD SWIM!!!

The crowd went mad.

Children screamed, parents hugged each other and clapped one another on the backs; some were even brave enough to wave their midge hats in the air so that for a moment the shore looked like a frantic rainbow. Cameras flashed and the TV cameras whirred into action. *Never* had there been such an exciting swimming race; never *ever* had there been such a surprising start . . . and such an eventful finish.

And it wasn't over yet.

I was just about to introduce myself to my mysterious friend when Joe started to shout.

'It's not fair,' he yelled two metres from the finish line. 'Ned's a cheat! *I'm* the champion, I want that prize! I HATE NED FINN . . . !'

Suddenly a huge, black, menacing shape with two large humps, a long neck, tiny head and three horns, rose out of the water. It circled to the left . . . then the right and *then* . . .

It dived.

Terrified, the crowd called out to Joe. 'Watch out,' they yelled. 'There's something behind you! It's a *monster*!' But Joe was too angry to listen. Amor Ron, sensing a chance for some good publicity, ordered his boat to rescue Joe.

'Let everyone know that Amor Ron Saves Lives!' he crowed, posing for the onboard TV crew. Just then the creature broke through the surface and, with a gentle flick of its tail, swamped the boat with a huge bow wave that cut its engine dead. Amor was soaked.

Meanwhile Joe, as oblivious as ever, hit the surface

of the water with frustration. Splash, he went. Splash, splash, splash, splash,

SPLASH!

He hit the snout of the mysterious monster.

'*Heeeeeeeeeeeeeeelp!*' Joe cried, as the creature opened its great jaws, gently scooped him up into its red mouth and tossed him into the air with a flick of its bright green tongue.

'*Aaaaaaah!*' he wailed, as he slid down the monster's neck and up and off one of its humps.

'*Yeeeeeeeeeeeeeeeeeeeeeeeeeeeeikes!*' he moaned as he was carefully – but precisely – flicked up into the air with the creature's tail.

Back on the shore, the stunned spectators cried out with terror. 'Help him,' they cried. 'Do something! Save the boy!' But then, as Joe continued to be tossed and twirled in the air, they decided that he wasn't in danger – he was simply taking part in the most dazzling display of aquabatics they'd ever seen. As one, the crowd rose to their feet and began to clap and cheer for Joe in earnest. 'Bravo!' they marvelled. 'This is wonderful, fantastic, superb!'

'Yes,' agreed the journalists. 'But where's Amor? How did he manage to organise such a brilliant publicity stunt?'

No one was interested in me or the race any more. All anyone wanted to do was watch Joe and the monster. Needless to say Amor Ron was almost beside himself with excitement.

'Yes,' he cried to the admiring journalists as, dripping wet, he finally stepped off the boat and on to the shore. 'You are right! This *is* my new business venture! My nose for money never lets me down! Forget fruit and vegetables, I hate the stuff. No, from now on I am going to start the Loch Ness Aquatic Circus – and Joe Blagg will be my star turn. Now – I'm starving. Can anyone buy me a burger?'

Unable to believe my eyes and ears, I turned to face my mysterious watery friend who was still lurking unseen in the shallows. 'Excuse me,' I coughed nervously, 'but . . . could you please, *please* tell me who you are?'

Chapter 24
CHAMPIE THE CHAMPION

His name, it turned out, was Champie – or Champ for short.

He came from Lake Champlain in Vermont in the USA and he was (if you can believe this and I must admit I wouldn't unless I'd met him) not only

a) Lucky's long-lost cousin, but also
b) a Plodothod
and therefore
(as accurately suggested by the museum)
A Loch Ness Monster!

'You see, Lucky's just that – Lucky!' explained Champie. 'He has cousins living in different lakes throughout the world. We are all Plodothods, all members of the same family, but over the years we've learnt to survive and adapt to our surroundings. Some of us are short and dumpy; others are skinny and tall; we're blond, brown, yellow, blue, pink with purple spots . . . you name it, we've got it! That over there,' he chuckled, nodding towards the creature who was currently bouncing Joe on its tail, 'is Ninki Nanka, Lucky's third cousin from Gambia. She's very hot on manners and asked Lucky to give her the chance to introduce your friend to what she calls *his better nature*! . . . Ouch! That looked painful,' he laughed as Ninki spun Joe on the end of her nose.

'Will . . . will Joe be OK?' I gulped anxiously.

'Oh, she'll only tease him till he apologises . . . And, yes! There he goes!' he laughed. Sure enough, I heard Joe's voice floating across the water saying, 'OK, I give in! I'm sorry I gave those Finns a hard time!!!'

'Don't worry, he'll be fine,' Champie assured me. 'Ninki never holds a grudge. But I think your friend might be rather tired by the end of the day.

She told me she was going to make him walk home – from the other end of the loch! That just leaves us with one other person to deal with – Amor Ron. This is the third time he's tried to exploit us Plodothods. The first was in a Siberian valley – we had to arrange for a flood that time. Then he tried to kidnap Lucky and now he wants to turn us into a circus act. Well, stay here and watch this!'

And leaving me sploshing about in the shallow water, he swam off stealthily to the shore where Amor was still talking to the press about his new plans. Arching his neck high above the water, Champie bent down and gently picked Amor up in his jaws . . . and shook him upside-down. Out fell a mass of sweetie papers, crisp packets and two (yet to be eaten) burgers. Disgusted, my new friend dropped Amor into deep water as the cameras flashed and journalists scribbled in their notebooks.

'Hmm,' said Mum, giving Dad a hug. 'There's less to Amor Ron than meets the eye. If you are what you eat, then he's complete rubbish!'

Champie slithered quietly back towards us, chuckling softly. But there was still something I needed to know. 'Where's Lucky?' I asked. 'Is he all right?'

'Don't worry, he's fine. He's with the rest of the family. They're all hiding out in some shallows at the other end of the loch, far away from prying eyes. Lucky was desperate to swim with you but we decided that, because he's only a baby, he really wasn't strong enough to tow you over the length of the loch. Tell you what, why don't we all go and see him?'

So Stacey, Bill and I followed Champie's directions to a secluded cove at the edge of the loch. Champie pursed his lips and gave a loud whistle. As if on cue a whole number of strange heads, necks, shoulders, humps, horns and tails poked out of the water.

Bill gasped. 'But . . . but how do you manage to hide yourselves when you're all so big?'

'Ahah, another trick of Nature! You see, as we grow older, Plodothods learn how to shrink in water. It takes a bit of time, but we can reduce ourselves to the size of a squirrel or a rabbit. It's a useful trick if you're trying to squeeze through those tight underground passageways that link our lakes with the seas. But we have to watch out for tap water. It tends to make us shrivel up rather too much.' He smiled. 'Lucky told us how small he became whenever he had a swim or a quick dip in your mum's washing up bowl. Must have given you quite a fright!'

'Yes,' I agreed, remembering Stacey's screech when she washed him in the bathroom. 'But Champie, there's still something I don't understand. According to Bill's books, dinosaurs never lived in water.'

'Those books are right – we didn't!' laughed Champie. 'We only changed our ways when man came along. It's a sad fact, but men and dinosaurs don't mix! However, though we now live in the water full-time, we *do* return to the shore to lay our eggs – which can be a bit of a problem. Once on shore, Plodothods swiftly grow back to their normal size. That's why we've been spotted so many times around Loch Ness. It's one of our favourite places – and we *love* the midges.' He broke off. 'There's Lucky,' he cried. 'Hey, Lucky, come over here and introduce Ned to the family!'

And after a great many hugs (and – though it pains me to admit it – poos, burps and farts), Lucky introduced us to his cousins. And they were all just like Lucky: smelly, bright, greedy – and wonderful.

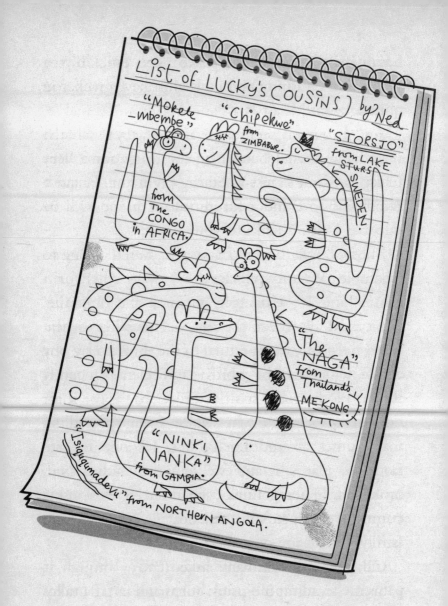

There were also loads of cousins from Lake Waitorec in Australia, Lake Manipogo in Canada,

Lake Blanco in Chile, Lake Kol Kol in the Dzhambul region of Kazakhstan, Lake Labynkar in Yakutia, North East Russia – even from China!

'And so you see,' said Lucky, after all the introductions had been made, 'I really am a very lucky dinosaur – just as Stacey predicted. I have a family, a home and a future full of friends. I'll be safe and well – thanks to you.'

'But how did they all know you were coming to Loch Ness?' Stacey puzzled.

'Ah,' replied Champie with a broad smile. 'Through ET or Evolutionary Telepathy. It's a neat way we've developed of communicating by thought as well as by words – which is very handy when we live so far apart. We Plodothods use it for everything: passing on facts and information, telling jokes and tracking each other's whereabouts. It's how we know when a new Plodothod has hatched. It takes a bit of getting used to – Lucky's just a beginner – but he's a quick learner and I'm sure he'll get the hang of it soon.'

'Can we learn it as well?' asked Bill eagerly.

'Sadly not,' apologised Champie. 'ET takes millions of years to develop. As far as I know we are the only species to have succeeded. We Plodothods live for centuries and some of our eggs don't hatch out for *years*. And I mean millions and *millions* of years. So if you see another cream egg with a bright pink kiss mark (the true sign of a Plodothod's shell), let us know! It's sure to be one of ours and we *love* an excuse to hold a welcome party!'

I shuddered at the thought. However fond I was of Lucky, I couldn't help thinking that one dinosaur in the family was quite enough.

Finally, it was time to go. 'Will . . . will I ever see you again?' I asked, hugging Lucky and trying hard to ignore the lump in my throat. 'I'm going to miss you so much.'

'Not half as much as I'll miss your socks, Ned!' laughed the dinosaur. 'And of course we'll meet again – how about next year? Then we can all swim together in the loch. But mind, Ned, when I say swim I mean just that! No aids, no floats, no tomato suit! Do you promise to keep practising?'

I promised.

And with that, the family of Plodothods waved their tails, bowed their heads and (well, if you don't mind, I think too much detail is unnecessary) . . . *whiffed* their way into the water and slipped off into the late afternoon sunshine.

Chapter 25
GOING HOME

It was 6 o'clock.

The sun was setting over the loch but the crowds, exhilarated by their exciting afternoon, still lingered by the shore. As I rounded some trees, I could hear Joe being interviewed by a TV crew.

'So, Mr Blagg, is it true that you have decided to swim across the English Channel?'

'No way,' shuddered Joe, who had just had to trudge ten long miles back from the wrong end of the loch. 'From now on I'm only going to swim in centrally heated indoor pools.'

I had just reached the steps of the hotel when Mr

Peaseby came stumbling out, shouting in triumph and waving an exercise book in the air.

I blinked and stared at him more carefully. Could I be imagining things? Was he really, could even *he,* be wearing a . . . a . . . *skirt?*

And socks?

'Well done, Ned, well done!' he enthused, pumping my hand up and down. 'That was the most marvellous swim – and win! Such a pity you were completely overshadowed by yet another of Amor Ron's *brilliant* publicity stunts. Do you know those monsters were so realistic that some people actually thought they were real! Ha, ha . . . some folk will believe *anything.* Not that I'm complaining. The race has been a huge success. Amor Ron is donating tens of thousands of pounds to the school funds and my name has never been better known! Why, one spectator said I was just like the Loch Ness Monster itself: unforgettable! By the way,' he added, giving me a twirl, 'what do you think of my kilt? A bit short? Stacey thinks I should wax my legs, but . . . there has to be some ceiling to the price of fame!'

Realising I was staring at him like a stuffed fish with my eyes glazed and my mouth wide open, he sighed and held out my exercise book. I gasped. It was my school project book – the one containing Stacey's Dino Diary.

'And talking of Stacey,' continued my head teacher, 'I have to say well done to you, Ned, on this *fabulous* piece of fiction. Your mother found it when she was packing up your room and handed it in. And don't worry; she *assured* me she hadn't helped you – not even so much as glanced at its pages. Of course,' he added, fiddling with his earring, 'this school project was supposed to be a factual work, but how can I fail to reward such a

remarkable piece of writing? A Dino Diary indeed! Your description of a Plodothod had me doubled-up with laughter. So we're going to give you a Special Prize for a Special Project. Shall I tell you what it is?'

I nodded, still unable to take my eyes off his knees.

'A signed copy of the first edition of *Dino Facts* by Professor Bron T. Saurus.' And without waiting for my reaction, he spun off, leaving me to groan in peace.

And peace it was. For now the crowds and the journalists had disappeared, the beautiful loch was as calm and tranquil as ever. In fact, there were only two jarring notes: the midges and . . . Dad.

'Hello, Plankton,' he cried cheerily as he came through the door. 'Cod a load of this! I found it on the shore. I believe it's a prehistoric fossil; otherwise I would never have *piked* it up. But – you won't believe this – when I first noticed it, I could swear I heard it going *cheep* . . .'

And opening his large clenched fist he revealed his secret:

A creamy white egg about half the size of Bill's hand . . . with a bright pink kiss mark on one side.

'UH OH!'

we yelled as we begged Dad to put it back.
And I'm sure he did . . .
Aren't you?

EGG-SIT

PS
FROM THE AUTHOR:

DINO FACTS AND NESSIE NOTES

Dino Facts

Dino Egg is a work of fiction. I made it up. The idea of a dinosaur being too lazy to hatch its own eggs and therefore causing its own extinction came into my head one day and wouldn't go away – and that's how I came to write this book.

But even though it is fiction, I still did lots of research into dinosaurs. I spent hours in my local library reading through books in the prehistoric section from picture books to encyclopaedias. And when I'd run out of books to read, I surfed the web. I became fascinated by these extraordinary creatures.

I also asked tough questions of some of the many dinosaur experts I met when I visited schools and I want to thank them all for their help.

My research threw up all kinds of mind-boggling facts and figures – though they are always changing as new discoveries are made. I thought I'd share my favourite Dino Facts with you here.

1. Dino Numbers

Experts think that there might have been about three thousand different types of dinosaurs. They've found the bones of about eight hundred of them, and at any time somewhere in the world, you can be sure that a determined palaeontologist[38] (an expert in dinosaurs) is scraping away at the ground in the hope of finding more. Apparently there are lots in Mongolia.

2. Dino Times

The Dinosaur Age lasted for one hundred and sixty-five million years. During that time, the climate changed about every fifty million years. It

[38] *pal-ay-ON-tol-o-jist*

was during the Cretaceous[39] Period (between one hundred and forty-four and sixty-five million years ago) that dinosaurs really came into their own.

3. Dino Menu

Some dinosaurs were plant-eaters (herbivores). They tended to walk on four legs, though some did walk on two. Meat-eaters (carnivores) ran along on two legs (presumably to catch up with their prey). Some dinosaurs (called omnivores) liked both meat and veg. The perfect dinner party guest!

4. Dino Society

Despite what I wrote in this book, dinosaurs and humans never mixed. However, we do live alongside birds, which are thought to be directly descended from dinosaurs. The animal which links dinosaurs directly to birds is the Archaeopteryx[40], which means 'ancient wing'. It lived in Europe about one hundred and fifty million years ago, at the end of the Jurassic Period. It was about forty-five centimetres long and had feathers, teeth and a

[39] *Cree-tay-she-us*   [40] *Ark-ee-OPT-er-ix*

bony tail. Other winged reptiles of that time are called Pterosaurs[41]. They are not classed as dinosaurs.

5. Dino Looks

Dinosaurs were strange-looking beasts. My personal favourites are Triceratops[42] (a plant-eater with three horns) and Euoplocephalus[43], a well-armed reptile that was covered in bony plates. Even its eyelids were shuttered by bone and its tail was so powerful that one swipe would have broken your leg. Hmm, reminds me a bit of Joe . . .

6. Dino Moves

Ned was right! While enormous dinosaurs roamed the land, huge reptiles called Ichthyosaurs[44] and Plesiosaurs[45] lived in the water. Scientists believe they were related to dinosaurs but they have never been classified as dinos. They had all died out by the end of the Cretaceous[46] Period.

[41] *Te-ro-saurs*
[42] *Tri-SERRA-tops*
[43] *You-OH-plo-keff-ah-luss*
[44] *Ik-thee-oh-sorz*
[45] *PLESS-ee-oh-sores*
[46] *Cree-tay-she-us*

7. Dino Sizes

New dinosaurs are being discovered all the time. One of the biggest is the Argentinosaurus[47] which might have measured forty metres from head to tail. But not all dinosaurs were giant monsters. Some, such as the Compsognathus[48] were not much bigger than a chicken.

8. Dino Deaths

No one is sure why dinosaurs died out. There are loads of theories: illness, famine, climate change, even UFOs! But many experts now believe that dinosaurs met their doom about sixty-five million years ago when a great lump of space rock called a meteor smashed into the earth. It created a huge dust cloud that blocked out the sun and caused the earth's climate to change dramatically with disastrous consequences.

Have fun looking up other facts in these dinosaur books:

Weird and Wonderful Dinosaur Facts by Monica Russo, Sterling Publishing Co. Inc

[47] *AR-gent-eeno-sore-us*
[48] *Komp-sog-NATH-us*

Eyewitness Visual Dictionaries: The Visual Dictionary of Dinosaurs, Dorling Kindersley

Did Dinosaurs Really Snore? by Philip Ardagh, Faber and Faber

Why, Why, Why Did Dinosaurs Lay Eggs? Miles Kelly Publishing

The Knowledge: Dead Dinosaurs, by Martin Oliver, Scholastic

You could also ask your teacher or librarian to recommend websites about prehistoric animals.

Nessie Notes

I've never actually seen the Loch Ness Monster, but I have a sneaking feeling that Nessie is down there somewhere in the depths of the loch. And it wasn't until I did some detective work that I realised that lots of countries have their own version of the Loch Ness Monster – they're all over the world! So, Champie is in America, Ninki Nanka in Gambia and Storsjo is swimming up and down Lake Sturs in Sweden.

Perhaps you know of others you can add to the

list? I like to imagine them partying along with Lucky in some remote and mysterious lake or loch somewhere in the world. Meanwhile, if you want to know more about Loch Ness, here are two addresses:

The 3-D Loch Ness Experience, 1 Parliament Square, Edinburgh, Scotland
The Loch Ness 2000 Exhibition, Drumnadrochit, Loch Ness, Scotland

But remember, if you see a prehistoric egg with a bright pink kiss mark, *DON'T BRING IT HOME* – or who knows what will happen?

Thanks

Finally, I couldn't end this book without thanking just a few people who have helped me: Lindsey Fraser my brilliant agent; Emma Matthewson and Georgia Murray at Bloomsbury for sharing my enthusiasm for the prehistoric past; my friends Caroline, Cathy, Katie, Cerys and Lee Weatherly; Jane Lucas at the Natural History Museum, and Rachel for her help in working out the number of seconds in a millennium.